THE INSUFFICIENCY OF MAPS

THE
INSUFFICIENCY
OF MAPS

A Novel

NORA PIERCE

"Forceful . . . unsentimental coming-of-age story."
—*Publishers Weekly*

WASHINGTON SQUARE PRESS
New York   London   Toronto   Sydney

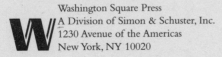
Washington Square Press
A Division of Simon & Schuster, Inc.
1230 Avenue of the Americas
New York, NY 10020

First Washington Square Press trade paperback edition April 2008

WASHINGTON SQUARE PRESS and colophon are registered
trademarks of Simon & Schuster, Inc.

For information about special discounts for bulk purchases,
please contact Simon & Schuster Special Sales at
1-800-456-6798 or business@simonandschuster.com.

Manufactured in the United States of America

10   9   8   7   6   5   4   3   2   1

The Library of Congress has cataloged the Atria Books edition as follows:
Pierce, Nora.
    The insufficiency of maps: a novel/Nora Pierce. — 1st Atria
    Books hardcover ed.
    p. cm.
    1. Quechan Indians—Fiction. 2. Mentally ill parents—Fiction. 3. Foster
parents—Fiction. [1. Racially mixed people—Fiction.] I. Title.

PS3616.I3565 I57 2007
813'.6—dc22   2006048029

ISBN-13: 978-0-7432-9207-8
ISBN-10:   0-7432-9207-3
ISBN-13: 978-0-7432-9208-5 (pbk)
ISBN-10:   0-7432-9208-1 (pbk)

For Joan Gruss

ONE

Our beginning, as far back as I can remember, my hand in hers. We're on the bus and we are short forty cents. Mami drops our fifteen pennies and they scatter across the floor of the bus. They roll under the seat of an old man in a dark green uniform with a ragged name tag on the pocket. He picks them up and carefully puts them in Mami's hand. "How much do you need?"

"Forty cents," she says.

He holds out two quarters. Mami says, "Go ahead, angel." I balance my way back to the driver and drop them into the coin slot. Mami takes my hand and we sit next to the man who gave us the money.

"Guess what?" She leans in close to him. "I'm getting married tomorrow. Going to the chapel." Her eyes grow wide. "Ding-dong, the bells are gonna ring!"

He grins, wrinkles cutting into the corners of his mouth. Then he winks at me, "Lucky man." A large woman seated across the aisle

1

from me takes a tissue out of her purse and gestures toward the little black bits of dried blood on my legs. I've been scratching little bumps for days. "Chicken pox," Mami says. But they look like mosquito bites. The woman looks Mami up and down, but Mami just smiles.

The old man eyes our plastic bags and muddy shoes. "Looks like you've come a long way."

"We're going home," Mami says. "My father moved us away to the city when I was as small as my little girl here."

We've been walking all day to catch this bus. We came from a place far away, mostly walking, and the world around us changed from pale gray and wet to red and dry. I can't remember where we were before we started walking, except that it was so bright and bugs made loud sounds and we slept outside and counted the stars. We drew pictures in the mud of how we would rearrange them if we could. It is this lost place I am dreaming about, leaning against Mami's shoulder when the driver wakes us.

"It's the end of the line," he says. "Where exactly are you trying to get?" Mami digs out a postcard, hands it over to him.

"Lenny's? On route nine? That's all the way at the other end of the line. On the number four bus."

Mami stands, gathers our shopping bags and says, "Transfer, please."

He shakes his head. "You can't transfer to anything out here."

She stares at him while the empty bus exhales black fumes. No one moves but me. I lean into Mami's hips and watch the smoke rings rise outside the window. "All right," he says finally. "Just stay on the bus."

When we do get off, it's late at night. The driver steps off the bus to point us in the right direction, and we start up the dirt road.

"Where are we going?" I ask.

"To the reservation to see your father," Mami says.

"When are we going to get there?"

"Don't know, angel."

"Are we going to have happy dream come true?"

"Yes," Mami says. "Happy dream come true."

She hangs a blue plastic shopping bag on her ponytail and sings, *"Wedding bells are ringin' in the chapel, ding-dong the bells are gonna ring!"*

She smiles, takes my face in her hands. "And you can be the flower girl."

"Yeah," I say, "and you can be the *other* flower girl."

Mami rips some weeds from the ground. "Like this," she says, and points her toes, prancing along the road, stretching her neck high. She flings weeds to either side of her. I tiptoe behind and throw little sprigs of grass in the air.

"You know what this means," Mami says. She races in a circle around me and mocks a donk on my head. "The condor fight!"

I fall over dead.

She scratches and scratches the air above me.

"Now my dear." Mami leans over me, making her voice shaky. "Now you are dry bones."

I open my eyes and look up at her. "Tell the story, Mami."

3

"All right," she says. "Late at night a condor swoops down from his cave, and carries off a young girl." As she speaks, I ride the air with my hands as wings. Mami picks me up and swings me around till everything blurs. She smells like cut grass. Her long hair is the color of water at night, thick and slippery on my cheek. The stars whoosh around. All around us the trees and phone poles are still and listening. When she sets me down, there is a swift movement on the road. Headlights. A purple arc of soft light spreads across her arms and she whispers.

"The condor takes the girl to the top of the mountain and hides her in his cave. But her grandmother finds her, takes her home, and hides her in a barrel. The condor comes to the grandmother's house and pokes at the barrel. He scratches and scratches with his talons. When the condor finally leaves and the grandmother runs to the barrel . . ."

We both mock horrible screams, covering our eyes and pointing to the barrel. We shout in unison, "Dry Bones!"

Lenny's Bar is just outside the reservation. It has a neon sign that spills pink all over the road in front of it like a crazy bunch of fancy-dancers in a scattered pattern. I dance too, pretending I'm one of them, showered in pink. Pink all over my arms, pink on my nose, pink on my cheeks, pink on the top of my head, crazy beautiful, kaleidoscopic pink melting into the gravel. And Mami and I dance in it. Up and down like war dancers in the sun. Pink, pink, pink.

Inside the bar it's almost pitch black. We walk through drifting webs of smoke as Mami searches for her groom. She walks right up to a man in the middle of a conversation with a skinny, stringy-haired white woman, and says softly, "Goddamn drunken Injun." He turns around and squints at her.

Then a big smile, "Amalie!"

Mami lifts me up, and sits me on the bar in front of him. "Sober up," she says to him. "You don't even recognize your own daughter." Then she looks into my eyes. "This is your papi," she says.

The stringy-haired white woman slams her beer bottle on the bar. "She ain't nothing but, but . . . a little bastard like her mother."

Papi's sleepy eyes round. He's trying to get a good look at me. But Mami reaches through us and slaps the woman.

Papi picks me up and we go out into the pink. A big splotch of it melts into the top of his long black hair. He puts me down and then squats to look at me with his black eyes. He puts his face up to mine, rests one hand on his knee. A beer is still sweating in the other.

"Well," he says. He smells like whiskey and cigarettes. "Are you a pretty angel like your mother?" I reach up to touch the pink spilling down his nose and cheeks. He laughs. Then I squeeze my eyes shut really tight and I dance for the ghosts all rising up around me, knees up, knees down, arms waving like an airplane. And Papi is laughing. He stumbles around behind me, singing *"hiya-howa,*

5

hiya-hiya, howa-hiya." He grabs me up and says, "Sure glad your mami came back to me." I break free and run around him, whipping up the dirt, singing *"Ding-dong the bells are gonna ring, ding-dong, dingidy dong!"*

Papi's trailer is made up of four rooms: a large living room with knobby orange shag carpet, a long hallway of yellow-brown linoleum with little bumps marking the intersection of rooms, a kitchen and bathroom, and a bedroom at the end of the hallway. I sleep in the front of the trailer in a closet-size room. The walls are plain paneling, except for a cherub that Mami has cut from the wrapper of an Angel Soft toilet paper package and tacked to the wall over my bed. It is so hot that the air seems to be tinted deep red. There is just enough room for a fan at the foot of my bed and I wet my head in the sink and push my face up to it to cool off. Mami doesn't seem to sleep anywhere. She spends all day on a lawn chair outside, talking to the old people and bumming cigarettes from any-one who walks by.

I want Mami to have a wedding, but she won't cooperate. "You're the condor," I say to Papi. "And Mami, you're the young girl." But we never get to the walking down the aisle part. Papi lifts Mami up and over his shoulder. "Good-bye Alice," he says. "We're off to the ears of the mountain." Then he carries her inside and they shut the bedroom door.

• • •

Since we are home now, the home Mami always told stories about, I'm going to throw away all of our bus tickets. I find them tucked inside a plastic shopping bag in the closet, a fistful of limp bus transfers and tickets, and I go outside to bury them. The dirt outside the trailer is hard on top, so that I have to use a rock to scrape through. But underneath, it is soft and moist. I push the tickets in deep, cover the spot with stones. I find an empty plastic bucket under the trailer. Little bits of sagebrush and marigolds swim in the dirty gray water. I drag it out and stand on it. I can see through the kitchen window, which is propped open with a fan. Inside, Mami and Papi are seated at the kitchen table, their hands linked, their heads leaning into each other.

Papi says, "Because I got this place when Old Auntie died, and anyway, I wanted to come back for us. It's a home I could ask you to come to, not some apartment full of a dozen other Indians and an eviction notice every ten months."

Mami's head drops a bit, her smile turns down. "What about that woman?"

"She don't mean nothing to me, Lee. It's you I want, you're the only thing I ever wanted."

He takes her face in his hands, kisses the top of her head. "I won't ask you any questions, Lee. I don't care where you been. And Alice. Look, this is our home, okay, all of us."

Loose strands of her hair fall out of the messy bun she's made, and Papi tucks them behind her ear. "Shit," he says, "we were young, right? All that stuff happening with you, it scared me. But there ain't nothing wrong with you except being away from where you're supposed to be. I just want you to know that I'm sorry I let you go. I still don't think it's right what they done to you. You don't need no hospital, no medicine. I'm sorry I didn't come, Lee." He covers his own face with his hands, breathes deep. "I'm sorry, baby."

I think, *What hospital? What medicine?* He holds her hard. It looks as if he is hurting her. He says, "You'll stay, right?"

The bucket bows under my feet, and tips over so that I bang my arm against the jagged aluminum steps. There is sharp pain, and then a prickly tingling, as if my arm is falling asleep. Mami comes out of the trailer, picks me up and holds me in her lap. She rocks me on the steps, blowing softly on the bright pink welts. I watch the peroxide fizz inside the scratches on my arm.

I am trying to have a vision dream, but I keep dreaming about frozen french fries that Papi buys from the rez store. They come in a blue-and-white package, cost sixty-seven cents, and take, Mami says, exactly eleven minutes to cook. Papi is gone all day, working, and Mami and I search each room for forgotten change, uncovering pennies beneath the linoleum, and turning over cushions, looking for nickels. One day we find almost a dollar, and Mami sends me to buy french fries. The drop-down freezer in the store is a mess of soupy melted food and limp boxes in icy water. I pull the package out of a shallow pool at the bottom, bring it up to my nose to smell, and then drag it across my forehead to cool off. The girl working at the store laughs at me. Her little fan whines from behind the counter. I run all the way home, but just as I get to the little gravel path in front of the trailer, I trip. The box flies in front of me and spills open. The soggy french fries roll all over and their ridges fill up with dirt. When I go in to tell Mami, she sits down on the couch and bites her lip. We go out together, pick them all up, and wash them in a colander.

When the evening comes and it cools off inside, Papi and I play Go Fish in the front room until we fall asleep on either side of the couch, with our legs still crossed and the cards scattered between us, but Mami never seems to sleep. I wake up when she turns off the radio and shakes a blanket out over us. Late at night, she carefully folds brown paper bags from Papi's Wild Turkey whiskey bottles and stacks them on top of each other in a drawer. She's saving crinkled piles of them for my lunches, even though I never take a lunch anywhere. In the morning, before Papi goes down to the road to wait for the work trucks, he finds them in the silverware drawer and piled on top of the pans in the cupboard.

. . .

After brushing my teeth, I walk out into the kitchen to find Mami draining hot water from the spigot into a mug of instant coffee. Her hair is all gone.

"I've got twins in my head, Alice, little girl twins." She rubs the back of her head. All the black hair has turned a fuzzy gray. "They told me to shave it."

"Twins?" I follow her into the bathroom. "Are they pretty?"

"I don't know," she says. "They sound pretty."

I climb onto the toilet to look into the mirror. We look alike, especially our eyes, though her skin is darker. Mami's eyes are always growing wide. I smile into the mirror, inspecting my teeth, copying the way I've seen Papi do it.

"Your smile is prettier," I say.

"Let me look." She turns my chin left and right. "Yours is shiny," she says. "Like the sun in the middle of the day. Like yellow bird feathers." She uses her thumb to pull my chin down and look a little closer. "Like an angel from God sent down to bless me."

I cup my hands around her ear and whisper into her head, "Can I shave mine, too?"

She cuts most of it off with the scissors first. Then I stand on the toilet and she whizzes the electric shaver around my head until it's all gone.

"You look like Kumastamxo."

"Kumastamxo!" I say. I wave my magic hands around the top of her head. "Go away," I command the twins. "Leave my mami alone."

It's too hot to stay inside the trailer in the afternoon, so I follow Mami outside when she goes for a cigarette. When I open the screen door, she jumps out from under the wooden steps and sprays me with the hose. I scream and duck, but she keeps spraying till I'm drenched. Then she falls over laughing, the green hose still convulsing, leaking little brown lines in the dirt and gravel. I grab it while she's laughing and spray, spray, spray. As I chase her around the trailer, Papi's truck pulls up. He sticks his head out of the driver's side window and stares. Our prickly hair, drenched from the hose, stands up in jagged patches so that the scalp shows through.

"What's this?" he says. "Are we joining the marines?"

I point the hose at him, "Kumastamxo!"

"It's the new style," Mami says. "Everyone in Paris is mad for it. Got a cigarette, handsome?"

Papi gets out and kicks the door shut with his foot. He holds something gently in his hands. Mami takes the cigarette from his mouth and he leans close to me so I can cup my palm over his. A tiny frog jumps into my hand. Ticklee! It jumps out and I chase after it.

TWO

Strange weather here. Dust devils everywhere, trees bitten down to stubs, and then, rain. So much rain that the irrigation ditch turns to slush, and all around us the cleaved earth creates mudslides. The aluminum roof on the trailer is so thin that when rain hits, it sounds as if we are trapped under the river rapids. Water rushes off the roof and makes long, skinny waterfalls. And along with the rain comes a horrible declaration from Papi's sister: school. She sits under a tarp outside with Mami and Papi, playing cards while I collect rain in little paper cups I found behind the rez store. I'm making a pond. Mami says that when I get it done, even though I've only dug about two inches so far, we can get fish to put in it. I offer her a cup full of mud and gravel, "Here's your sundae. Please come again soon."

Mami says, "But I ordered a cherry." That's when Papi's sister leans over and scrapes the mud off my cheeks and ruffles my short hair. Now that it's growing in again, it itches whenever someone touches it, so I swat at her hand. "Aren't you a feisty little boy," she says, "making mud-pies?"

"A pond," I say, "for fish. And anyway, I'm a girl." She tilts her head and pulls me close to her under the tarp. I'm barefoot with no shirt, and a thick layer of mud coats my arms and knees. She smells like vanilla and alcohol. Where her eyebrows should be, there are just two drawn black arches. She's Indian but she wears blue eye shadow and she has a perm. I reach up to touch her eyebrows and a clump of mud falls into her lap. It's diluted with rainwater so it spreads quickly and leaks down her legs. "Alice!" Papi says. But she just takes my hand and says, "It's okay, we'll go in and clean it up." It's hot inside the trailer, and I run to push my face up against the fan, but she comes at me with a washcloth. She wipes up all the mud and then puts me in the tub. She looks behind my ears and in my mouth, and inspects the little spots that have come back.

"Chicken pox," I tell her.

"How old are you, honey?"

"I'm five."

"What do you do all day?"

"I'm trying to have a vision. Plus dig a pond."

"Nobody has visions anymore," she says, "that's just old-people stuff."

"Mami does."

She wraps a towel around me and pulls me out. "Nonsense," she says, and then takes me to the screen door where she leans out and says to Papi, "You might think about getting this child registered for school."

Mami looks up through the veil of her cigarette smoke. "Fuck school," she says.

"I don't like it," she tells Papi later. He stands over the sink smoking, ashes falling into the trails of water around the drain and melting.

"It's just school, baby, they'll take care of her."

"She's still too young for school."

"She's five. That's perfect."

Mami sits on the couch and picks nervously at the lint on the crocheted throw. "I don't know."

"It's on the rez, Lee, it ain't like it used to be, like boarding school. They're even teaching them Quechan. It's Injun fever over there, I tell you."

The next morning when I wake up my clothes are laid out at the foot of the bed, along with one of the crinkled brown paper bags Mami has peeled from Papi's whiskey bottle. At the kitchen table is a plate of french fries with a candle sticking out of the fattest one. "Make a wish," Mami says.

I wish I don't have to go anywhere. Then I blow out the candle.

After a few moments of the radio droning, and the faucet dripping, I cry, "But Mami, why won't you let me stay with you?"

Mami tilts her forehead to mine. Her pretty cheeks are wet.

"I know. I want you to stay."

"Don't cry," I say. "I'll stay here with you."

Mami cries harder. I rub the damp hair around her ears. The heat from her face makes her cheeks pink and warms my fingers.

"But Mami, my pond's not done."

"I'll dig some for you." She pulls the candle out and we eat all of the french fries.

School is on the reservation. Outside the office, Mami's hand begins to sweat in mine. I look up and see that her face is all flushed and little glassy droplets are angling down her forehead.

"May I help you, then?" The receptionist is plump and Indian with pretty eyes buried in her cheeks.

"I'm here to register my daughter."

"Do you have her enrollment card? Her birth certificate?"

Mami starts to wobble, her bottom lip rattles. Pretty Eyes looks at me.

"Yes ma'am," I say, and hold up the ID card fastened around my neck.

She touches Mami's arm gently, leads her to a chair. "She's had her inoculations?"

"No, I don't think so."

Mami looks panicked. She bends to me, whispers, "I'll wait for you here, *m'ija*. They can't make me leave."

After giving Mami a clipboard of forms, Pretty Eyes takes my hand and we go down a narrow hallway, through the thick wood doors of an empty classroom. "Don't worry," she says. "Sister Joanne's to be your teacher and all the little kiddies love her."

"Mister Joanne," I whisper.

"Sister Joanne."

"Is she your sister?"

"Well," she smiles and bends to look at me, "I guess we're supposed to think of her that way."

Pretty Eyes writes my name on a paper tepee and pushes a safety pin through it. She eyes my red spots suspiciously so I pull my sleeves down to cover them. Then we go to another classroom where she knocks on the door. A woman opens it, takes the slip of paper Pretty Eyes holds out for her. She looks so strange in a black hood, a princess in a long dress!

"Children," Sister Joanne says. She tugs me to the front of the room where a whole group of kids, more than I've ever seen at once, is looking at me. She looks at my little tepee. "This is Alice." So many faces follow me to the back of the room, a spot on the big yellow carpet. "Today," she says, almost in a whisper, "we are taking a trip back in time to learn about our history." She points to a picture she has hung from an easel. *Indians dancing. They are all gray. Where is the color?*

"Let's think of some things we will need for our trip." A small boy sitting next to me raises his hand. His hair is mussed into a perfect little tuft just off the center of his head. His face is wide and

17

dirty. "I have a leather water canteen that my father gave to me." Sister Joanne smiles at him. "That would be very sensible, Abel."

"I can go home and get it," he offers.

But Sister Joanne says, "This is a special kind of journey. The kind we take in our imagination." She stretches the word *imagination* out so slowly that I realize it is magical. Why does she say it like that? She should keep it a secret, like the words Mami sometimes says into the mirror or to no one at all. The words I can't catch.

You are tall and pretty and magic. I love you, Sister Joanne.

"I have a pond," I tell her. "You can get water from it."

Sister Joanne says, "Alice, you will have to try to raise your hand"—she wiggles her fingers in the air—"like this, whenever you want to speak. That way everyone gets a turn."

Abel looks at me. I put my face up to his, our noses almost touching, like Mami does, say *pop!*, and we start giggling. He covers his mouth, and then tells me to shhh! Now we have to move to a little table with chairs, so I ride my condor wings to the other side of the room. But then someone's hands are on my arms. Sister Joanne's? She gently pushes them down to my sides. I hold them stiff and straight while seated at the table.

Sister Joanne hands out construction paper and scissors. "One of the most important things we'll take on our trip is a feather-dress." She puts a loop of construction paper on her head.

The girl seated next to me has her eyes fixed on me. I pull a wad of green leaves from my mouth to show her. She smiles. The leaves go back in warm. But now Sister Joanne's hand is on my chin. She's telling me to spit it out. As I lean over the trash can, she whispers, "What *is* it, dear? Don't you know not to put things in your mouth?"

"Chewing leaves," I say. Sister holds my mouth open and looks closely to be sure it's all gone. Without it, I feel shaky and hungry. It's a strange, nervous feeling.

Sitting with us at the table, Sister explains about a dance, a ghost dance where all the Indians died in a great battle like the condor fight. Her eyes are kind, and when she talks, she smiles at each of us.

And then there is food! In a little cardboard box. Abel peels the top off for me and inside there are little compartments with hot mashed potatoes and shiny buns. I eat all of the mashed potatoes and hide the bun in my paper bag for Mami. I want to take some for Papi, too, but instead I eat the rest, the whole thing, and feel sick.

Abel holds his hands out, pushed together in a praying position. "Here's the church," he thrusts them into my face, "and here's the steeple." He opens his hands and waves his fingers all around in front of my eyes. "Open the doors and here's all the people."

It's so funny!

He points to the picture I wear around my neck. On the back Mami has written her name, my name, Papi's address, my grand-mother's name, and a code of numbers and words to protect me.

"Is that your mom?"

"Yeah."

19

"She's pretty."

"I know."

"Are you going to come to our school now?"

I think about it, decide, "No."

"Wanna see something?"

He pulls out a leather wallet with a picture of Charlie Brown embroidered on the front. He flips it open and pulls out a dollar bill.

"So."

"Watch this."

He pulls on the dollar and it grows longer and longer, until I see that it's lots of single dollars all taped together.

He stuffs it all back in.

"Watch this."

I put my paper feather-dress on my head. Some of the construction paper got crushed so a few strands hang in my face. I put my hand to my mouth and undulate. Then I start jumping around and Abel shoots me with two side-holster guns. I make like he got me in the knee. I start chanting, "Wounded knee, wounded knee."

A teacher is leaning over me, her hand raised to hit me. Everyone stops and stares, scared for me. I've never been hit before and I wave the construction paper from my eyes and stare back in horror. She comes closer, her eyes narrowed and mean. Her bottom lip twitches.

"Mami?" I search the giant room for her.

The teacher stoops down and pulls the feather-dress off of my head.

"My mother, your mother, and you are Native."

Mami never calls us Native. We are Indian or Indio or Quechan. She crumples the paper strands into a tight ball in her fist.

"Don't make fun of us."

Outside the school building, Mami is passed out right in the middle of the schoolyard, her feet sticking straight up and ten little Indians staring down at her. Their paper feathers are floating around them like blossoms falling from trees.

"Miss Black! Miss Black!"

Pretty Eyes rushes over and feels Mami's forehead. "Oh God, she's passed out."

I crawl through the Indians and kneel beside her head. I put my nose on hers and whisper, "Mami, wake up!"

When nothing happens, I wave my arms around, "Kumastamxo, Kumastamxo!" Her eyes pop open. Pretty Eyes helps her up and all the kids stare at us.

"Thank you," Mami says to the receptionist. "Now, Alice, let's go home and dig."

THREE

I have seen this woman before, I know how she walks, and what she carries in her suede brown briefcase: lollipops, all orange-flavored and wrapped in sticky plastic. I've seen her in the school hallways. Sometimes she sits at the back of Sister Joanne's class and stares at us. When I look at her, she smiles eagerly. Other times she talks to Abel, or calls out for one of the other kids when we're gathered together around the creek behind the school building, digging up roots and replanting wildflowers. Once, Abel and I fished up a dead minnow and were burying it in the mud when I spotted her watching us. She wore a pilled knit jacket and skirt, though it was too hot for us to even wear our T-shirts. Sweat eased down her forehead and cheeks, drawing lines in her makeup, and even from so far away, I could see where it pooled in her collar. Now I see that her eyes are the color of weak tea, as if they were not steeped long enough and her pale blond hair does not move at all in the hot winds.

She follows me home, stands at the edge of the road, close to where I have buried my paper feather-dress. I am counting paces and marking X's in the mud when she bends and waves to me.

"Hey, little one," she jiggles her hand, a strange, hesitant wave. "What are you doing there, burying treasure?"

I squint at her. The bright sun is making a halo around her face, so I squat down and unfold my map to shade my forehead.

"Look," she points to my shoe. "It's untied." She comes closer and gathers the frayed laces. "You forget this a lot?"

I shake my head. Ashamed, I confess, "I don't know how to do it."

"It's easy, just make one loop, two loops, and put them together. See," she says, when a bow emerges. "Easy."

She rests her handbag on her stomach, hugging it to her. "Can I ask you a question?"

"Okay."

"Why weren't you in school today?"

"Mami said it wasn't safe."

"Do you live here with Joseph?"

I don't know who Joseph is. I frown at her. "I live with Papi."

"Tell you what, next time I see you, will you talk to me about it?"

"Okay."

She folds a lollipop into my hand. As she walks away, the rustling birds in the trees nearby caw and rearrange themselves. Abel crawls out of the bushes.

"You shouldn't talk to her," he says.

"Why not." I hold out my lollipop. "Look what she gave me."

"She can make you disappear."

"No she can't."

"Yu-huh. She gets kids adopted out. She got our cousin. Just ask my brother."

"What's adopted out?"

He pushes me in the chest and I fall over. "Poof," he giggles, "you're gone, Charlie Brown."

"Liar."

He stands up and waves a twig in my face. He's tied a thread and a goldfish candy to make it into a fishing pole.

"Let's fish in your pond."

"I'm busy." I fold up my map and go back to counting paces.

"Why are you always digging?"

"I'll show you." I make him pinkie swear. "But you can't tell anyone."

I lead him over to my tree and uncover the things I've found. I hold up a piece of ribbon, a bead pelt, and from deep in the dirt, a sponge doll with one arm missing. She wears a buckskin shawl and ribbon dress. "Fancy Dancer," Abel says. He flutters her shawl like butterfly wings.

A horn sounds from a truck on the highway.

"Oh no! Bury her," I say. "Twins are coming to steal her."

Abel squeals. He buries the doll and lies on top of the dirt, spreading his arms out to protect her. His hat falls off.

"Help," he screams, "we're getting adopted out!"

I melt like the wicked witch of the west. "Aah-uh, she's adopting me!"

I put Abel's hat on.

"You can't be a cowboy!" He sits up.

"Why not?"

" 'Cause you're an Indian."

"So are you."

This gives me an idea. "Bury me!"

It takes the rest of the afternoon to dig a hole big enough to lie in, and then Abel just sprinkles dirt over me, and all my limbs stick out. But I stay there after he's gone, pulling up handfuls of dirt and sprinkling them all over me. The dirt feels good, cool in the heat. I close my eyes and watch bright yellow spots float on the back of my eyelids until I've fallen asleep. Late in the afternoon, a shadow wakes me up. It's Papi.

"What are you doing?" he says.

"Rooting."

"Rooting?"

This makes him laugh hard. When he's finally caught his breath, he pours some beer around me. "Well, let me water you."

I giggle.

Papi sits cross-legged beside me. "You can't root literally, baby doll." He kisses me on the forehead. "Come on, now."

He lifts me onto his shoulders, grabs my bare feet around the ankles to steady me.

"You got to . . . shoot, baby," he laughs some more. "I guess you got to look around real close. It's when you get to knowing a place so well that you see all the stuff other people can't see, that's when you're rooted."

"Mami said we came back for our roots."

"Did she? I thought she came back for true love?"

"Nope. Roots."

"Well then, we best get our roots home and cleaned up."

"Can we have french fries?"

"Again?"

After supper I go back outside to meet Abel near the bushes. We can see Papi backing away in his truck. Mami opens the screen door and calls after him to "Get a bottle of bourbon, too."

"Exactly how many fish live in the river?" Abel wants to know. We've been an hour trying to catch a puffer fish for my pond, when there is sudden noise from the trailer. Someone is knocking on the screen door.

"Open up, Joseph."

I follow the sandy path behind the trailer, inch my way underneath and hide. Above me, I can hear Mami walk to the door. The floorboards squeal and squeak and little bits of wood dust rain down on my head. Abel inches in behind me. There is the sound of glass breaking, a bottle cracking apart on the gravel out front. Mami has thrown something out the window. When the pieces scatter, I inch myself farther under the trailer.

"Bitch," the voice says. I peek out and see that it's the stringy-haired woman from the bar, the one who called me a bastard. Her freckled skin has mottled splotches all over. "Fucking squaw," she says. "Dirty-ass Indian." Above us, Mami is turning things over, rolling something, pounding against the linoleum. We can hear her running. Something else—a bottle—flies out the window.

Then the sound of Papi's truck. We watch his feet as he stumbles in a drunken zigzag up the gravel path, carrying a paper bag full of beer.

"Elvia?" He looks at the white woman. "What the hell?" He ducks and a whiskey bottle lands by his feet. Mami runs down the steps, letting the screen door slam behind her. She runs straight for the woman and pushes her to the ground. Then she tries to pull the woman's hair.

"Hey!" Papi says. "Quit it now!" But when he tries to pry them apart, he slips and falls face forward.

They both look at him, staring for a long while before the white woman gets up and slaps him. Then something funny happens. Everyone starts giggling.

"They're all drunk," Abel whispers.

Mami helps the woman up. Papi just stares, blinking stupidly. "What?" he says. "You're friends now?"

They just laugh at him. This makes Abel start to giggle. I reach over and cover his mouth, but Papi peers under the trailer.

"Heya," he says. "What are you two doing under there?"

"Sneak us a beer," Abel says.

Papi laughs. "I can*not* sneak you a beer, Abel, your mother would kill me."

"Please?"

Papi sits on the steps and opens his beer. "All right. I'll give you a sip if you come out from under there."

Abel crawls out and sits next to Papi, but I stay under the trailer. The white woman crawls over to the trailer, peeks under, her face serious. "I'm sorry," she says. "I'm sorry I called you a bastard, honey."

"You're welcome," I say. They laugh at me. Papi and the white woman. I crawl out and sit on the steps next to Mami. I touch her face where her eye is bruised, and then look back at the woman. "Go away," I say. But Mami puts her arm around me and pulls me into her. "Shh," she says. "It's okay, angel."

The white woman's shirt glows a pale blue: she's in the headlights of a police car.

"Oh shit," Papi says. He shields his eyes. "Someone called the cops on us."

The police car makes a crackling sound on the gravel as it pulls up to the trailer. The driver's window rolls down. "What's going on, Joseph?" says the policeman.

The white woman tries to get in her own car. She says, "I was just leaving, Officer." But he gets out and takes her keys, opens the back door of the police car for her. "Get in, Elvia, I'll drive you home."

NORA PIERCE

"Who called on us, Jimmy?" says Papi.

The officer doesn't answer, but Papi looks through the passenger-side window, then walks back toward the trailer. "It's that snooping BIA social worker," Papi says. Then louder, "She can kiss my ass."

I try to shield the lights in my eyes but Mami's arms are around my chest and she's carrying me into the trailer. She opens the closet and pulls me in, her arms so tight on me it hurts. In the darkness, I can hear her breath, swift and laboring. Her hands are digging into my shoulders, nails sinking into my flesh. It's hot inside the closet and I'm aware of my breath and the insulated quiet. We can hear Papi shut the outer door. "Going to bed now," he calls through the screen. "All nice and quiet."

"Cut the light," he whispers to Abel.

Mami draws me closer, and there is a long silence before Papi says, "She's leaving, Lee. Hell, girl, come out of there." I think of the two white women outside in the police car, of Mami's quick breath above me, of orange lollipops.

When Papi opens the closet, my fear turns to anger.

"Shhh," Papi lays his arm on my shoulder. "It ain't nothing. She don't belong here, that woman, that's all."

"I'm sorry," I say to Mami. "I'm sorry."

Mami goes to the window and presses her face against it. I stand behind her, watch the woman pause beside the police car. The night paints her deep blue. She bends to retrieve something from her purse, and then gets in the car and shuts the door.

"See," Papi says softly, "she's leaving, honey."

When the car pulls off, I go out the screen door, call up all the meanness inside me and kick up the dirt so that it sprays a cloud in front of me, thrust my arms through and whisper, "Kumastamxo!" The dust falls as I wave my hands. "I wish you would *die*."

Mami catches my hand in the air. She stands behind me, her breath swift above me. "Careful," she says quietly. "Careful, baby."

FOUR

Papi has a new job. He's helping with the dig just outside the reservation where they have found all sorts of things in the dirt. He says they are building a new floor for an old common house, and renaming it Yuma Museum. Sister Joanne says there is going to be a visitors' center and offices for the anthropologists. Already they sell woven juncus-leaf pendants and old photographs. Tourists come to look at baskets, at the broken pottery and dusty skirts on the shelves. Papi is paid to work on the dig, helping to pick through a mound where they think death offerings and bones are buried. Papi shows me the maps they've drawn and hung on the walls, the drawings and pictures of hidden bones and settlements. But Sister Joanne says they are not so old, those bones. "Your gramma's gramma," she tells us in school. But how can two hundred years not be so old?

I hang around the bottom of the hill while he's working, trying to get a look at what they're doing.

Where he digs, there are sticks wrapped with ribbon sectioning off a patchwork of turned earth. There are white paint buckets everywhere filled with rocks, and wheelbarrows full of dirt. Lying about in the mud are small egg-colored shells in the shape of birds. I lean far over the wooden fence, trying to see closer. Papi comes to stand beside me.

"Bones," he says to me.

"What happened to them?" I ask.

"What happened? Nothing, that's just what we look like underneath."

He knocks on my knee, and it makes a hollow sound that surprises me. Then he picks up the little bird, and leans against his shovel. He holds it up to his face and blows on it, before stretching it out to me.

"Feel," he says.

But when I touch it, it is hard, no feathers, nothing soft like I expect.

"Hey, cousin," someone calls. A man with long, loose black hair is shouting from the top of the hill, shouting at Papi. A group of men wearing hard hats stand around him, leaning on their shovels. "Hey, you're digging up your uncles, man." He shouts at one of the workers, spitting in the dirt nearby.

Papi drops the bird in my hands. "Keep it."

I watch his boots sink into the mud and kick it up as he walks up the slippery hill toward the group of men, sending pieces of stone and dirt rolling behind him. But I put the bird down gently, and rub the soft dust from its tiny, featherless head.

"Who the hell are you?" Papi says at the top of the hill.

"*I'm* the American Indian Movement." He hands Papi a brightly colored flyer. "Who are *you?*"

Papi doesn't answer. He holds the shovel a little higher, poised behind his shoulder.

"Red Power, man. Haven't you heard? You ain't got to let them walk all over us anymore."

A young girl appears behind him. She is dark and pretty. Bright blue dragonfly beads hover around the edges of her long braid. "He doesn't mean nothing," she says. "He's just drunk." She holds her hand out to Papi. "Inez."

"Ain't you going to introduce yourself, Lester?"

Lester says, "I'm Les." Then he addresses all the men and boys standing around. "We'll be at Lenny's Bar tonight, you should all come." Inez smiles pretty, her eyes on me briefly as she walks away.

As I walk back home, I finger my elbows, wondering if it's true that that's what's underneath.

I ask Mami at home if it's true about the bones in the ground.

"Where do we come from?"

"The mountains."

I point to the sharp edges of red in the distance. "Like that hill over there?"

"Yep. But bigger."

"Is Papi digging up his cousins?"

"I don't think they're Quechan bones, angel."

"Why?"

"Because Quechans have always burned their dead."

"Then what are they doing?"

"Mining. At least they were until they found the bones."

"The birds?"

She looks up from the potato she's peeling. "What birds?"

"The bird bones," I say.

"No," Mami says. "Bones of an old, old man. Ancient bones."

She puts the knife and potato down, goes to the window and draws the curtain. "Dry bones," she says. "Poor bones."

"Poor bones," I say.

They take me along to Lenny's Bar. We park next to a spray-painted VW bus. Papi tells Mami that they all live inside it, all the AIMs. There are eight of them, three girls and five skinny boys. Mami stacks pillows and sleeping bags in the bed of the truck for me, and tucks me in. But I can't sleep, so I sit up and try to see in through the window of the bar. I can smell it from all the way out here in the parking lot: a warm caramel smell of smoke and sunburned sweat. When the door swings open, I duck down quick. I peek over the tailgate and see that it's not Mami, but the pretty, dark girl from the dig.

I say, "Hey."

She comes to the truck, leans on the tailgate. "Hey," she says. "Who are you?"

"Alice."

She shakes my hand. "Inez." Up close, I see that a yellow-and-white daisy is painted onto her cheek.

"I like your flower," I say.

She sits on the bumper of the truck and rolls up a spicy, green-grass-smelling cigarette, then licks the paper. "Come here," she says, "I'll paint you one."

I scoot closer. She takes a paintbrush from a suede purse she wears crossed over her shoulder, and two little sealed cups. She licks the soft end of the brush. "Hold real still," she says and tickles my nose with the soft brush soaked in yellow.

"Where did you come from?" I ask her.

"New York."

"Can I see?"

"It's kind of far, little cousin."

"Like, if we walked it would take us two *hours*?"

"A little more than that. You and me are in the west and that's in the east."

"Are you Quechan, too?"

"No, I'm Shinnecock. You never heard of us?"

"I've heard of Mexicans."

"People have forgotten Indians are even around in New York.

37

Where I come from, all the white people live in these big houses that are empty all winter. Us Indians live right next door, but nobody notices."

She dips the brush in the other cup, holds my face in the cool palm of one hand, and leans in close to paint small dots onto my nose. I look away, try to concentrate on the neon sign, so that I can hold still and not squirm at the tickling.

There. Beautiful. She takes a pocket mirror out of her purse to show me. A little fat daisy has sprouted on the tip of my nose. I smile into the mirror.

She wants to know where I would go, if I could go anywhere in the world. I pull my knees up to my chest, fit them inside Papi's oversized shirt, and chew on the beads around my neck. "I don't know," I tell her. I can't figure out any place I want to be. Only who I'd want to be with.

"People say us Indians ain't supposed to get wanderlust—that's when you got ants in your pants, and you just want to see every-thing. We're supposed to love the land we've lived on all these thou-sands of years, and blah, blah, blah, but it don't seem to me like we have anything here, not anything we could really call *ours*. Every-one's all mixed up now, anyhow. Don't you wonder what it's like in the rest of the world?"

"No."

"I do. I got places to go."

I prop my head on my elbow. "Aren't you gonna miss your mami?"

"She died a long time ago, coming home drunk in my auntie's car."

"Did she die for good?"

"Well, she ain't haunted me yet."

"Did you miss her?"

"I missed her bad."

"Were you crying?"

"Oh, I was crying, crying a bathtub full, crying an ocean."

She starts coughing. It's a terrible scraping sound that starts in her throat and echoes in the parking lot. Then she holds her head with both hands. "You know what I'm gonna be, Al? I'm gonna be Miss World." More coughing.

"Did you know I was Miss Indian World? Well, I'm gonna be Miss *World* World, not Miss little Indian World. And they're gonna have to fly me to Brazil, or Paris for the finals."

"You're not gonna be in the American Indian movements anymore?"

"You know, the problem with me is I don't just want it all back," she giggles. "I want it all back with interest. I want the old ways and the new ways, too. Before I met Les, I never thought of myself as an Indian. Even on the reservation, next to all my old uncles and aunties, on the same land where the Shinnecock were born, I just felt like a leftover, like a ghost. I never thought about it his way."

"What's his way?"

"Take it all back. Be Indian like old auntie in there—that sort of thing. Hey, I like your haircut." She flips through her magazine, shows me a page with a short-haired skinny girl. "You look like her. Twiggy."

"I look like Kumastamxo," I tell her.

"Right," she says, lying back on the truck bed and blowing smoke rings straight into the black sky. "That's exactly what I was thinking."

FIVE

Old Tia Jimenez's great-grandson is dead. Mami says he has come home from Vietnam in a casket, and his greatgramma had to ask for him to be buried here, and not in a special cemetery in Arlington, Virginia. There is going to be a funeral tonight, and all afternoon, Papi has been standing in the doorway, drinking beer and smoking. For a long time, he hasn't noticed me sitting on the steps next to him. The early night sky is alive with wind. Far off, a fire is burning, a single oak torch in the night. It looks like a rip in the night sky, where the next day has spilled through.

"Is that the funeral?" I ask him.

"It is."

"How come there's a fire?"

"Because when you die, your coffin gets burned up. All your clothes and shoes and stuff, too."

"Does it hurt?"

41

"No. You get your face painted and you get all gussied up in new stuff and everybody sees you off right, giving you presents and maybe singing to you, and then when you're right cooked," he ruffles my short hair with his fist, "we cover up all the ashes, and bury you good."

"That is sad, Papi."

"Nah. This is probably the best party Willie's ever been to. His old gramma knows how to throw a going-away party."

"Are you gonna miss him?"

He smokes quietly, then flicks his cigarette off into the gravel out front. His chest heaves once, but he doesn't answer. He just leans down and scoops me up, lets me rub the hair behind his ears while he smokes and smokes in the night. Mami has gone to help make food for the funeral, and it seems like Papi doesn't know anything. "Don't I have to take a bath now?" I ask him. He says, "Get in the tub and scrub all over." When I come out, with a halo of steam around my head, he says, "You forgot to wash your face." So I get back in. I'm in for a long time and my fingers are all pruned when he finally pulls me out. When he leans into me, I can smell the sweet, sharp liquor on his breath. He squeezes too hard when he picks me up, but I don't say anything. He helps me get dressed in the clothes Mami left out for me, and then he smudges us with his cigarettes, three lit at once, waving them around us like a bundle of burning sage leaves, and laughing.

"I'm just foolin'," he says. "I don't got nothing to smudge us with. I guess we'll have to smudge at the old house."

"What's the old house?"

"An old house that's been around for as long as anyone can remember, so old it don't even have a floor, just some dirt."

We walk together, Papi in a new shirt and me in a dress that Mami has pinned all over with ribbons. The funeral is on the other side of the hill, past the dig where Papi works. He warns me not to ask him any questions about the dig tonight. "Some people are not too happy about it. But we ain't digging up any more bones, anyhow. It's just some old baskets and some trash."

"What if you do?"

"Do what?"

"Dig up bones?"

"Listen, little woman, when you grow up, do as I say, not as I do, all right?"

He lifts me onto his shoulders and tickles my bare feet.

"No shoes again?"

"I hate shoes," I say.

Papi laughs. "Yeah, me too. You know who else hated shoes?"

"Who?"

"Willie Jimenez. If they put shoes on that smart-ass I think I'm gonna have to take 'em off."

At the old house, everyone is standing outside holding paper plates and beer. There is a crowd around a bundle of bright clothes and replanted skinny trees. The fire is lit and people are throwing things onto the bundle, which keeps sinking.

43

Abel has a bowl of beans that he is trying to toss into the trash can from the corner. Whenever his papi looks, he pretends to be eating them. Sister Joanne is here, and Abel's father and the bone-digging men.

I ask Abel, "Is Willie Jimenez in that bundle?"

"Why do you want to know?"

"I want to know if he's wearing any shoes."

"Oh, brother!" He yawns, dragging his feet as I pull him along. We try to get a look, but too many people are crowded around.

Inside, Tia Jimenez is sitting in the only chair. Her skin is burned-looking, and her face appears smooshed. One by one, people are shaking her hand or kissing her on the cheek. She kisses the women and pats some of them on the shoulders. But when the bone-diggers talk to her, she slaps them on the head and they laugh or look sorry. I hide behind the trash can, where Abel's beans are landing. I've collected some of the beans and try to dunk them into the trash can when Papi spots me. He takes my hand and walks me up to the old woman.

"Say hello, Alice."

"Hello," I say.

She just nods. But even when I look away I can feel her eyes on me. She has long gray-white hair, a face dark brown–colored and carved with a network of deep vertical wrinkles and crisscrossing tattoos. She's very fat, in a skirt of bright ribbons and a deep red shawl. She leans into me, her eyes searching my face, and takes my chin in her hand. She turns it left and right, squeezing firmly. It hurts, but I keep my eyes wide open.

"Nyi'vak vasawk," she says to Papi.

She takes my face in both of her hands again, rough hands that feel like sandpaper. She smiles broadly, nodding yes, yes, and waving Papi away. Her breath is warm and wood smelling, but I don't try to get away, I just stare back. Maybe I hate her. Maybe I don't. When she lets me go, she laughs loud.

Papi squats so his face is next to mine. "Someone's got to watch the fire, make sure it dies down all right, cover up the ashes, remember?"

"You do?" I say.

"You have to watch the fire?" Abel interrupts. He has stopped throwing beans and stands beside us with his papi.

"Crazy old woman," Papi laughs.

"Don't matter, does it?" Abel's papi says.

Papi kicks at the dirt, looks over at Tia Jimenez sitting solid on her chair. "Around here, *she's* what matters."

"Yeah," Abel's papi says. "But you wouldn't be the first to wonder how many marbles she's got left."

Papi takes my hand and we go outside. Up close the bundle is bright and hot, and makes the night all around look even darker. I ask Papi, "But *why* do you have to bury the ashes?"

He kicks at a log. "See this? Even after a rain, it's all dried out and eaten up, it would light up like a matchstick if the wind kicked up. Somebody's got to watch it."

Papi goes back to the trailer for blankets, saying the fire is so big, we'll be here all night. When he's gone I watch the arrowweeds collapse into the grave, smoldering and sending up curly lines of smoke. Abel sits with me for a while. It is so hot that no matter how far we sit from the fire, I feel like I'm burning up.

"You can wear my hat tonight," he says. It's a new hat from his uncle. A soft Stetson. But when I put it on, he keeps looking at it, and before he goes home with his sister and father, he says, "I might need it tonight, though."

Papi comes back with fuzzy blankets and he and Mami spread them out and sit with me. I rest my chin in my palms and watch.

Sparks and tiny twigs are flying, making popping and sizzling sounds. I pick up a blackened cone that has dropped nearby.

"What's this?" I ask, rolling it toward the fire.

"Pinecones," Mami says. "They split open, and send out all of their seeds. They can't do it without fires."

The pinecone rocks on the edge of the pit, then falls in.

"Think he can feel that?" I ask.

"Who?"

"Willie Jimenez."

"I'm pretty sure no."

"Maybe we should give him some water."

"That ain't gonna help much," Papi says.

"Do you think he's sweaty?"

"He's dead, baby."

As people leave, they say "good luck" and "keep watch" and "don't stay out too late." A short-haired woman gives me some thick tortillas and a handful of candy. Some of the men come by, too, and Mami makes me stand up and take their hands.

"Be a good little helper, you pay attention now."

"Okay," I tell them. "Jeez!"

I try hard not to fall asleep as the fire flickers down to lazy smoldering, and I watch drowsily as Mami and Papi dig handfuls of dirt and toss them onto the ashes.

Walking home in the half-light of early morning, Papi pulls me up to his chest, and the crunch of his footsteps on the ground litter, the rocking rhythm, sends me to sleep.

In my dreams, all the shoes in the world are burning up, and I'm inside the fire with Willie Jimenez, trying to run back to the mountain, but the ground is hot, too hot for us. I wake up having kicked so much that the flannel blanket is braided around my feet. I'm dressed in one of Papi's old button-down shirts.

Papi is asleep on a torn flannel sheet on the sofa, stained yellow-brown with spilled beer. His black hair is fanned out around him, and he's holding tight to the edge of the mattress as if it were a raft in the water. Mami is curled up beside him, weaving his hair through her fingers. Papi's face is all straight lines and angles, sharp

47

cheekbones and jagged features. He is the color of peeled tree bark, like the logs at the edge of the fire.

I peek at them through narrowed eyes. Papi stirs, opening his eyes for a moment, and pulls Mami in close. She is crying and her cheeks are shiny, making Papi's hair damp.

He says, "What's wrong, baby?"

She tells him something has been following her. Everywhere she goes, she can smell this thing behind her, the smell of wet feathers and decay. She says she talked to Tia Jimenez about it. The old woman said, "Sing a bird song, girl, remember your mother, that's all." But it wasn't. It would not go away. She rolls away from him, wiping her face on the sheet, and asks, "Do you think there are ghosts in the fire?"

"Amalie, there aren't any ghosts. It's that shit they gave you at the hospital, you're sad for other things, right? They messed you up in there. You were just sad, that's all."

But Mami cries. "It says we don't belong here anymore."

He gets up and stands by the door, his hands spread open at his hips as if he will keep her from leaving. My ears burn. He says, "Don't go again, Lee."

She stands, too, the blanket falling to the floor beside her, I can feel the soft edge of it on my feet.

He says again, "Baby, you don't got to go."

When she takes a half-step back, he winces, turns away and slams his fist into the wall. The paneling bows from top to bottom, and cracks in the shape of an X. His shoulders shake. Then it's quiet for a while. She goes to him, wraps her arms around his, resting her forehead between his shoulder blades.

"Okay," she says. "You're right, we should stay."

But later, Mami takes a beer and her cigarettes out to the front of the trailer. I get up and stand next to Papi where he sleeps on the sofa. I put my hand on the spot between his shoulder blades and it is strong and damp. His hair and back are slick with sweat. I say, "We won't leave you, Papi." On the steps, Mami is quiet, staring at the empty road. She lets me sit beside her, wrapped up in a sleeping bag. The sky is dense with light, so many stars crowded against one another; it looks like the night is too small for them. How will they get out? I imagine they will hold hands to become morning.

Before Papi wakes, Mami packs a blue plastic bag with things from the kitchen. Frozen french fries, cold fry bread wrapped in foil, bowls of congealed bean soup. Then she gently lifts me from the doorway. "Stand up, honey," she whispers. "We have to find your shoes." I stand, lean into her. I'm so tired, I want to fall back to sleep, and almost do standing up. She pulls me up and I wrap my legs around her waist. Then she feels around the floor with her feet until she finds my shoes.

Outside, the morning is still. It is a long walk to the other side of the hill near the common house.

Inez answers the door. Tia Jimenez has been teaching her how to weave juncus leaves. Inside, Mami speaks to her in a halting mix of Diegueño, Quechan, and Spanish. She tells again about the smell of damp feathers, the poisons and ghosts, the birds everywhere. Tia Jimenez lays out a thick pile of shawls and blankets for us on the kitchen floor. I curl up in a shawl and Mami rubs my back. Tia Jimenez sings softly, a quiet bird song. Her kitchen smells of damp mesquite flour and tobacco. She sits in an armless metal kitchen chair, stays there all night, singing and sewing until her head falls onto her shoulder and she snores.

In the morning, Inez takes her work outside, sits on the little porch. "You know," she tells me, "Willie Jimenez built this porch." All day, Inez ties ribbons together, sews beads onto belts and pendants. She rolls a thin cigarette and shares it with Mami. Mami smokes it, lies on the porch with her eyes closed, blowing smoke rings and talking with Inez. Inez's eye is a mottled black-blue color from where Les hit her, but Mami tells me that she must be already starting to forget. She says that Inez talks about how his stomach feels when he sleeps next to her, that she weaves long feather ornaments to braid into his hair, and that she gets drunk every night. "She misses him," Mami says.

"Where did you meet him?" Mami asks her. I'm tying ribbons around a tree and Mami and Inez are picking seeds out of a tangle of weeds on the porch steps. Inez says, "In a bar. A bar in New York City. He had this shirt on that said 'American Indian Movement.' I thought, what the hell is that? Some kind of program to *move* us all again."

She licks the rolling paper, and burns the end with her lighter. "'AIM's is coming,' they were shouting all over the place, came right up to me and said, 'You're an Indian!' like it was news to me."

She laughs, and it sends her coughing. She passes the cigarette to Mami.

"Hell," Mami giggles. "American Indian *movement,*" she stands, "I got that right here." She sways back and forth, twirls around with the cigarette.

Inez puts down her beads, and rests on her elbows, with her knees still crossed. She says, "Gimme that joint."

Mami passes it to her. "You ever miss home?"

"I suppose. I miss some things."

"You miss Shinnecock land," Mami says.

"I miss people, not dirt."

"Same thing."

"Think like that, you'll go crazy."

"I can't go somewhere I already am."

"Shut up, okay? Shut the fuck up." Inez holds out the joint, "Here, smoke this."

Mami sits down cross-legged with the cigarette. "I met Joseph in a bar. Christ, he was wearing that same red T-shirt, that Motocross decal was already peeling off. Someone had beaded the seams of his jeans, so I thought he had a girlfriend. But it didn't matter. Just looking at him, I knew he was mine. I figured, 'Well, it's settled.'

"He was shooting pool. He ran the table, sunk the eight ball in five shots. When he came to get a beer from the bar, he said to me, 'Well, if it isn't a real and true Indian princess.' Then he knelt right down in front of me, grinning, and kissed my hand. I told him, 'Royalty is for white people.' He laughed so hard the cigarette fell from his mouth."

This makes Mami and Inez start laughing. "He got me drunk on some cheap rye." They are laughing so hard Mami's words come out in fits and starts. "Oh God, making love to him was like groping my way across a room with the lights out. I just held on in the dark."

"Shit," Inez laughs, "what the hell are we gonna do, Amalie?"

We are in Inez's rusty blue Nova, on our way to powwow to sell the beadwork, when Papi comes. His clothes and breath are soaked in sweat and whiskey so that we can all smell him in the breeze. He leans in through the car window, looking past Inez in the driver's seat, past me in the middle, fixing his swollen eyes on Mami. He holds on to the rim of the door as if he will keep it from moving, and lodges his feet in the dirt under him so that his body leans against the car.

"What are you doing?" he says. His voice is calm. Mami doesn't answer.

"Hi, Papi," I say.

"It's just for a while. For protection," Mami says slowly. "The smell—"

He hits the roof of the truck with his wrists and then looks at

Inez, to see if she will chide him for hitting her car. But she closes her eyes, leans her head back, as if she were going to rest through the storm. Papi's eyes go toward Tia Jimenez. Without turning his head he says loud enough for her to hear, "There's nothing *fucking follow-ing her!*" Tia Jimenez stays behind her screen door, still as furniture.

He says softly, "Are you leaving me, Lee?"

Mami is quiet. I look at Papi's eyes, afraid he will cry.

But he looks as if he's just noticed I'm here. His body shakes. He says, "Al's in school, Lee, what about Al?"

Inez's eyes drift to Papi's hands wrapped around the window rim, his hips pressed against the door. She looks him in the eye. "We got to go, Joseph."

"Lee," Papi says. "Lee?"

Mami gets out of the car, walks around to meet him, and sags into his chest. He rests his chin on her head and sighs. I try to get out, too, but Inez blocks me with her arm. "You're staying with me, Al. Your mami needs a little time."

All the way to the powwow, I fold my arms up and stare out the window. I won't answer Inez when she asks me what I want to eat or whether I need to go to the bathroom.

But when we park behind a long line of buses, and I don't recognize anything, I can't help crying. "Are you taking me away?" I ask her.

"No, don't worry, Al." She pulls me onto her lap and squeezes. "You're not going anywhere. Just back home is all."

SIX

Mami is restless and Papi is getting worried. He follows her around almost everywhere, and starts coming home from work to have lunch with her. If she takes a walk down the road, he puts a hat on and follows after her. If she gets in the tub, he shuts the door and sits on the toilet the whole time she's in there. They even have a fight, when Mami says she's going to the rez store, and Papi wants to go with her.

"Stop trailing me. I can't take it anymore!"

And Papi says okay, but he sits on the stoop and watches her all the way there. Just before she gets to the little gravel path where I spilled the french fries, I watch her turn so Papi can't see her. She bites her fist. When she gets home, Papi throws his arms around her, hugs her hard, and then picks her up and carries her into the bedroom. When he's asleep, she comes out to watch me dig my pond.

She keeps asking Inez, who sits on a lawn chair beside her, if she should stay so I can go to school. Inez always gives the same answer, and Mami always agrees.

"Probably, Lee, you should stay if she likes it."

"Yeah," Mami says, "you're right."

Then more seriously, "You think so, huh?"

"Yeah, s'pose so."

"You're right."

I dig down seven inches and fill the pond up with the hose. As soon as it's done I lie in the grass and close my eyes and listen to the crickets buzz. Inez's rolled cigarette smells warm. "Time for some guppies," she says, waving away the smoke and mosquitoes from her face. But I don't care about fish. I just want to dig another pond. Sometimes Mami comes and lies beside me and asks me what I think about Papi and school. She talks to me in the same way she talks to Inez.

"Do you like it here?"

"Yeah."

"Do you think we should stay?"

"Yeah."

"You're right."

She turns to face me, reaches out to my cheek. Her eyes look round and scared. "You think God wants us to stay?"

"Yeah."

"You're right."

I fall asleep in the grass beside my pond and wake up cuddled under Inez's shawls. Mami stays up most nights, pacing back and forth in front of the trailer, smoking her cigarettes and putting them out, one by one, by the screen door, until a little molehill forms. She sits down when she's talking, her legs crossing and uncrossing, but as soon as she's finished speaking, she has to get up and walk again.

In the early morning, when the first lines of color are crossing the sky, I put Inez's beaded headband in my spiky hair. Mami laughs so hard I take it out and pull on my hair to make it grow. But Mami says, "You look beautiful." I follow her into the trailer. While Mami paces around the kitchen, I sit at the table with my chin in my hands. "What should we have for breakfast?" she says.

"Fry bread and french fries," I say. Mami melts lard in a pan and dips the fried dough in sugar so the edges will be sweet and crispy. But when she sits across from me with the potatoes, her eyes look glassy. The grease pan is bubbling over. The flame is up so high that it makes a steady whooshing sound, and grease crackles and spits out of the pan. It smells sweet and smoky. I watch Mami as she goes back to the stove. Burned bits of dough fly out of the pan and stick to her wrist. She puts the tongs in the fryer, pulls out the last bits of fry bread, drops them into the sink, spreads her fingers, and then dips her left hand, palm down, into the whooshing pan. She squeezes her eyes tight and bites her bottom lip.

"Mami!" I shriek. But her eyes stay shut, her head bowed and quiet as her face goes wet with tears. She winces, and then dips her hand back in, knuckles first. Little clouds of gray smoke twirl up from the pan as if she's just extinguished her cigarette. This time I throw my arms around her waist, choking as my throat knots up and hot tears surface.

"Mami," I cry, *"please."*

Her hand is poised above the pan. I let go of her, open my mouth wide and scream until my ears ache and Papi wakes up and runs into the kitchen. When I'm out of breath, I suck in air and then scream again until Papi starts shaking me.

"Make her stop!" I say. "Make her stop! Make her stop, Papi."

Mami reaches out for him. Her hand is a deep polished red and watery blisters are already surfacing on her wrist. Bits of burned skin are curling up on her hand. "They told me to," she says. "They told me to do it."

"Who?" Papi says. "Who told you to?" He's breaking an ice tray over the sink, throwing handfuls into Mami's hands. "Oh fuck," he's saying. "Fuck, fuck. Aw man, baby, hold still."

She leans into his chest and they slide down the front of the sink, in a heap together on the floor. Papi pets her head. Mami sobs and shakes and Papi wraps his arms around her tight. They rock together slowly. He kisses her neck, her hair. "Jesus, Amalie," he says. "Come back to me, baby, come back."

I watch them from behind a kitchen chair in the corner. Mami looks at her swelling, grated hand as if it doesn't belong to her, and then around the room as if she has never seen anything in it before, and then at me—right past me, as if she doesn't even know me. I get up and kick at the screen door over and over until it finally pops its little latch and lets me out. Cool air, dark, cicadas screaming. I run to the back of the trailer next to my pond and lie in the grass.

Dry grass pricks my ears and scratches my legs, and I look up at the sky, counting and counting the stars until my eyes are heavy and I hear what sounds like a rattle, seeds in a gourd, a far-off sound of quick and heavy movement coming closer and closer until finally I can feel the dirt and gravel whipping up around me and spraying my eyelids and cheeks. And then it flies over me, darkening everything around me, huge black wings and a smooth, slow landing until the bird—a condor—hits the grass on the opposite side of me, feet first, and then screeches to an awkward stop and folds its wings in. When next I know anything, it is the smell of Marni leaning into me: fry bread and shampoo. She winces as she pries me from the grass with one hand and lifts me into her arms. She wraps Inez's shawl tightly around my shoulders and rubs my back through the fuzzy crocheted fabric. I rest my chin on her shoulder and count the steps widening the distance between the trailer and us. The morning air is wet and crows are scattering as we walk down the gravel road, away from the reservation forever.

SEVEN

Bright noon on the side of a dry, empty road. Mami draws a tic-tac-toe board in the dust with a stick. She makes an O in the center and then hands me the stick. But I'm not talking to her.

When a truck appears in the distance, she holds her arm out. Her thumb, wrapped in a dirty, bloodstained bandage, points up. The truck pulls way ahead of us, taking a long time to stop. I slowly sound out the letters on the license plate holder. In red, covered in mud, they spell out C-A-L-I-F-O-R-N-I-A.

Mami starts toward it, but I cross my arms and stare off into the empty stretches of road. When she notices I haven't moved, she comes back for me.

"*Hijita?*"

I stare up at the sky. Clouds are condors flying back to Papi and Abel and two and a half ponds.

"Angel, listen to me," she says. "We'll make a new home with grampa."

But I don't care where we're going—I've never met my grandfather. I want to go back and finish my pond. Mami suddenly hugs me, and she does it so quickly that I can't help the giggles escaping. She squats to look at me. Her eyes are like river stones, a polished, still black. I try to look through them, to look into her. "You love those twins more than you love me," I say.

She looks past me, down the road to where an old sign is falling off its rusty post. "No." She roughs up my hair. "Angel, I left them there."

We walk together to the truck. Mami tries to lift me onto the seat, but I hold my pinkie out. "Promise?"

"Promise."

I climb up into the truck. On Mami's lap, I look through the open window and count the phone poles whizzing by.

"Kumastamxo," I say into the wind. "Stay away from Mami, no twins allowed here at all! Or else swish, pop, I'll shoot you with an arrow!" The poles are going by so fast; I wonder how far we are going. How long would it take us to get back?

"Poof!" I say, "we're home!"

I want to stay awake, but I'm so tired from walking in the heat. *Eyes,* I think, *stay open!* When we come back, I'll play cards with Papi and build a new tunnel for water from under the trailer. I'll dig all the way to the pond. I'm so sleepy. *Eyes,* I think again, *stay open!*

. . .

I wake to a sudden rain pounding the truck windows, running in little torrents along the frame. The windshield wipers are furious, squealing back and forth. Inside the truck, the air is moist and the windows are steamy. Mami has fallen asleep. I look at the truck driver; his skin is light pink and he has a red mustache and beard. I lean forward; try to wipe a spot clean on the windshield.

"I can't see," I tell him.

"Me neither hardly," he says. "It's pretty bad."

He puts a cigarette out in the ashtray and uses his sleeve to wipe the windshield in big circles. I look around for his horn, hoping he will pull it for me. "Are you taking us all the way to Grampa?" I ask.

"I'm going to Los Angeles," he says.

"Grampa went there on the Indian Vacations Act."

"*Relocations* Act," Mami whispers. Her eyes are still closed.

"Is that so?" the driver says. He pulls on his wiry beard, wipes the windshield again.

"Will this truck float?" I ask.

"I expect not."

"I think this is a flash flood," I tell him.

"Is that so?"

"My teacher told me about them. They come out of the sky like a big wave, and drown cars and people and houses, anything that gets in their way. Probably even this truck."

"No," Mami says.

"Is this a flash flood?" I ask her.

"No," she says. "It's just a storm."

Her voice is so low I can barely hear her, her words overly pronounced and slow. She pulls me closer and rubs at her eyes. The truck driver slows and then stops completely in the middle of the road. Ahead of us, some headlights are visible. When the driver wipes the windshield again, I can see that it's a car facing the wrong way. It's stuck between a bent mile marker and the muddy side of a small hill, which is breaking off in clumps into the water. Water rushes around the wheels. Through the windshield wipers, I see a woman in the driver's seat. She waves at us frantically. Another car is stopped diagonally in the middle of the road, its front end crumpled and its bumper detached and lying in the road a few feet away. The driver puts a baseball cap on and gets out of the truck. When he's gone, Mami says, "Sit tight, angel." She opens her door and slips out into the water. Her feet swoosh and when the door swings wide on its hinges, rain pours into the truck's cab.

When the door is closed again, I scoot forward, kneel on the seat, wipe a spot clean, and lean my forehead on the window. I can see a plastic bag blow against the window, beat against it gently, and then fly off in the wind.

I see the truck driver talking to the woman in the car. He comes back a few minutes later and calls the police on a radio in the truck. "Bad accident," he says. "It's this rain." He fits his hands under his armpits, takes them out, blows on them, rubs them together, and fits his palms back. He says, "Where's your mother, little one?"

I point to the side of the road. Mami is standing very still, her face tilted skyward. The rain has pressed her hair and dress close to her body, so that she looks like a statue in a fountain, water pooling around her legs. She lifts her loose tank dress over her head, and drops it. It floats a few feet away in the water. Her brown breasts are naked, dark brown nipples small and wet. She lifts her arms up, smiling. I look back at the truck driver to see what he will do, but he just watches quietly. She's naked when she comes back, dripping water from her soaked hair onto the seat. "It's beautiful outside," she says, pulling the passenger door closed. She lifts me onto her lap.

The truck driver says, "You okay, Miss?"

Mami squeezes me, smiles. Dreamily, slowly, she says, "Sure."

"You got a cut," I say. Ribbons of watery pink blood are running down her bare legs. "Look, *hija*," Mami points across the road. A shallow pool has formed by the side of the road and three tumbleweeds have joined together and are swirling around in a circle between some sticks and the mile marker. The sun is beginning to come through the thinning clouds. Wind chases the weeds around the wrinkling water.

Mami's wet legs are soaking rain through to my shorts, her damp hair dripping on me. I shiver, and she wraps her arms around me tighter and rests her chin on my head, breathing hard. The driver looks away, through the window. His hands tap nervously at the dashboard. I watch the rosary hanging from his rearview mirror swing gently back and forth.

When the police arrive with a tow truck, they give Mami a blanket to wrap up in. The driver turns the truck heater on for us. I sit on Mami's lap, and she rubs my back through the blanket. I watch the tow truck clearing the cars; the truck driver's outside talking to the police. Every few minutes, they both glance toward us in the truck. Finally, the policeman comes around to hold an umbrella over us, waits for Mami to pull me onto her hip, and walks us to a sheltered bus stop on the side of the road. Under the cornice, we're shielded from the rain. It drips on either side of us, dampening the rough brown edges of the blanket where it drags on the ground. The policeman rubs the back of his head, looks down at Mami's thin ankles. In the gray light, her skin is a smoky wood color.

The policeman looks us over. "You got family here?"

"No," Mami says. "In Los Angeles." A sound clicks on from his belt, a muddled, crackling sound of a female voice. It clicks off to quiet, clicks back on.

"Can we drop you at a hotel then?"

Mami says, "We don't have any money for a hotel."

He turns again to smile at the other officer. I play with the beaded choker around Mami's neck, working my pointer finger underneath it. She is still quiet, her eyes focused inward.

The policemen discuss us. "Why don't you give a call to First Baptist, Bud, see if they got any room?" Bud lifts the little radio attached to his belt.

"We'll take care of you," the younger one says, winking at Mami. "No worries."

He smiles at Mami strangely. "They can be pretty full there, though. We'll just have to see what we can work out for you."

Mami sets me down. "Wait here a minute, angel," she says.

He puts his arm around Mami and leads her back to the police car.

"But where are they going?" I shout at the policeman.

"Now hold up, little woman," he says. He cups his hand around a lighter and holds it to a cigarette. His face has gone red. Smoke spirals out of his nose and mouth as he laughs. "Trust me, it won't take long, baby girl." He reaches down and winks, pretending to pull a quarter out of my ear. He tucks it into my shirt pocket and says, "Your mama is a beautiful girl."

I lean on the bench for leverage and stomp hard on his foot.

EIGHT

I wake when the police car stops, warmed by Mami's arms and the forced heat coming up from the floor. Through the window I see a huge gray church.

"Here we are, ladies." The young officer hesitates for a moment, smiling at Mami. "They'll fix you up good in there."

We enter the church through the back door, and go through double doors into a big auditorium. The air is thick and hot. It smells like mildew and sweating bodies in here. Some parts smell like a dirty bathroom. There is a big kitchen with two stoves and a giant, steel refrigerator. Mami wears a loose flannel shirt and a mismatched skirt that she picked from a box of donations in the church office. Lots of people are standing around waiting. They are mostly gathered around a television propped up on a chair. We stand near a pregnant woman. Her tummy is huge, like a great big hill grew out of her. She wears a grubby housedress and an apron. But it won't tie around the hill, so its two ends are safety-pinned together. When she smiles, her eyes disappear into her pudgy cheeks.

She can't speak any English, so she keeps asking Mami, "What's going on? What'd they say? Who's that?"

But her baby knows some. He wobbles over, says, "Give me money!" and chases when I run away, thrusting his hand out to me. "Give me money!"

No! No!

He falls down and sits there trying to tie his shoelaces together. He's almost got it when she picks him up and slings him on her hip. The diaper makes a squishy sound against her skin.

The TV screen won't stay steady. A dog catches a stick and then flip, flip, flip. The image rolls around in the TV. After a while, people start going up to the kitchen where a woman scoops food onto plates for them.

"Spaghetti?" she asks. "Or franks and beans?"

Spaghetti or franks and beans? Spaghetti or franks and beans! I jump forward and back. *One potato, two potato!* "Hot potato!" I shout. The little baby giggles. *It's funny, his giggle-spittle.* "Hot potato!"

Mami takes my hand as we approach the line where a woman puts noodles and spaghetti sauce onto our paper plates. The plates sag and little oily rivers weigh down the paper and drip onto the floor. "Spaghetti or franks and beans!"

Another woman pours juice into paper cups for us. She smiles at Mami, says to the woman next to her, "You want to feel bad with all of these babies in here, but you can't stop them from being kids. They don't know it ain't a party."

"Spaghetti!" I tell her. "Or franks and beanzzzz!"

We take our plates back to a small room where there are a few cots tightly wrapped in rough gray blankets. Inside, a woman holds her baby's feet, lifting him up to slide a diaper under, and looks up for a moment to nod, and say, "I'm Ida."

Mami lies on one of the cots. She crosses one leg over her knee and shakes it emphatically. The *mujercota* sits on the cot beside her, working the knobs of a little radio she's plugged in between them. I sit beside Ida. She lets me lift one of her braids to admire the blue-and-white beads fastened to the end. Her eyes are yellow-green daisies settled delicately onto her cheeks. She has a coloring book, and in the spaces in between the lines, she draws me shapes, triangle houses with long, long driveways that snake all over the page. She draws rows and rows of flowers along the path to the house.

"Can you draw a fish?" I ask her.

She takes up another crayon, red, and draws an M with a big circle stuck to it.

Mami begins to sing along to the radio. She gets up and sways her hips to the music. Ida looks disapprovingly at Mami's hand. It has swollen slightly, a deep purplish brown stains her palm and winds in little freckly scars around her wrist and fingers.

"You runnin' from a man?"

"I believe in true love," Mami says. "Do you believe in true love?"

71

"Like in the movies?"

Mami sighs. She says, "Have you found your true love?" She starts singing: *"A love, a love, a love you don't find everyday-ay."*

"Girl," Ida says, "you're crazy ain't you?"

Mami laughs loud. She pushes her face up to mine and repeats, "Girl, you're crazy ain't you?"

"As a loon," Ida comments.

Ida tilts my face up and looks at me closely. "What, y'all Indian or something?"

"Uh-uh."

"Well, hell," she laughs even harder, *"no wonder!"*

Mami takes the *gordita* by the arms and pulls her up to standing. Her big breasts bounce on top of the hill. She giggles, revealing two missing teeth, and then as Mami spins her around, she grows red and covers her mouth with the palms of her hands.

"Shoot, little one," Ida coos to her baby. "This pretty little thing here done lost her mind."

"Hay-ah!" Mami says, and the two of them link hands and glide around the room. After a bit, they let go of each other and the *gordita* sits on the edge of a cot while Mami dances alone. I watch as Mami closes her eyes and very slowly sways her hips and arms. Then I close my eyes, too, and stand and try to feel what she feels, try to dance as happy as Mami. I spin around, spin a web of sticky lines to Papi's trailer, to Sister Joanne, to this little room and Mami, to the church and its constellation of colorful windows. I twirl around and around

fast until I connect up my whole life in a thin silvery web like a spi-
der's snare, and then I fall back and catch myself in it. I lie down and
watch the room spin around me. Ida hums and Mami sings the
words. Then the little boy trips over me and we laugh and laugh
until it hurts, and I roll on my stomach and rest my chin on my
hands to watch Mami. Dancing with her eyes closed, it seems she's
holding tight to something.

In the morning, we wait in line at the Red Cross, where Mami
can give blood and we'll get nine dollars, a cup of orange juice, and
cookies.

I wait in a plastic chair while Mami taps her foot in line. The
room smells like whiskey, like early morning, like newly unwrapped
alcohol swabs. The line moves slowly, and I'm tired. A man the color
of caramel sits next to me.

"You're a pretty little one," he says. "How about you run away
with me?" He leans down and gives me a wink. "I'm running from
the law."

"I can't," I say. "I go to school. My teacher's name is Sister
Joanne. Do you know her?"

"Hmm, let's see, does she wear a black veil and a long black
dress?"

"With white?" I gesture to my collar.

"Yes, that's the one."

"What's that stuff on your head?" I ask him.

"My rollers."

He feels around his hair. "Oh no!"

"What?"

"Oh no, no," he whispers. "It's gone."

"What's gone?"

"Oh, my bobby pin." He leans close. His eyes move quick and afraid. "I lost it, and I need it so bad. I really need it."

"I'll help you find it." I pet his arm. "Don't worry, sir."

"They'll be able to know what I'm thinking." His tears are coming quietly. "Oh God, they'll get into my head."

"Tell them to go away," I say.

He looks down at me, wet-eyed. "But I try to."

Mami finally returns with a miniature white stack of gauze stuck to her forearm, a dark red circle soaking through. She takes a sip of the orange juice they've given her in a Dixie cup, and then gives it to me with the stale chocolate cookie. Mami is smiling when she unrolls the nine dollars she got from the nurse and tugs on my cheek. "How 'bout pancakes?" she says.

I take the man's hand. "Can he come, too?"

Mami sits down and shakes his hand. His cheeks and chin are slick with tears. "What's the matter?" she asks.

He makes his face blank and shakes his head. "Nothing."

"Do you want to eat breakfast with us?" I ask again.

"All right," he says.

NINE

The first thing I notice about my grandfather is his hair. It hangs down in one long braid and bumps up against the small of his back where a length of suede is wrapped around it like the rattler on a snake. He stands sideways in the doorway, tugging at the rim of his cowboy hat—pushing it up, pulling it down, taking it off and running his hand across the top of his head to smooth his hair, and then fitting it back on. From the half-open doorway, he looks us over.

"Well, you're here then."

I crane my neck back to where the streetlamps stretch behind us. Their light shimmies across rows of houses, all piled against one another and ending in an alleyway littered with plastic bags and broken glass. July is burning the concrete. I slip my foot out of my sandal and touch the sidewalk lightly. It's gritty and brilliant where the street tar is soft and black.

Grampa takes Mami's arm, *"Mamuyo, miñe?"*

"Ihan Menya t'apa."

He looks down at me. "That means welcome home. I can bet your mami doesn't teach you these things."

"I hate you."

"Well," he laughs at me. "We'll have to start someplace and that's as good a place as any."

We just stand there, leaning against each other and swinging our bags.

"Well, come on in then." He opens the door to two tiny rooms piled high all around with shawls. There is a little table with a dusty sewing machine, a large sack of mesquite beans and dried bark. On top of a TV is a cradleboard, a pile of shawls, and a black-and-white picture of a woman in a turtle shawl. She holds a basket of bread loaves baked with tiny dough faces and pointed hats. They each have two little coffee beans for eyes.

I stretch for the frame, but can't reach, so Mami pulls it down for me.

"Bread babies," she says. "They're magic. When you were born, your grandmother, do you remember her? You used to call her Mamita. She made a little bread baby that was you. Only we didn't know where to put it. You don't have an earth shrine, so we couldn't feed it. In the end, Mamita put you out there in the street."

"Just bread," Grampa says. He looks at her oddly.

"Well, it seemed right to me."

"It's a waste. Do you know how often Carmen went to bed hungry? *We* went to bed hungry? And you two taken to feeding the intersection." He waves his pointer finger at me. "Don't waste your food, little one. Think of all the poor little traffic lights going without!"

"If you don't feed the earth, the earth won't feed you," Mami says.

"You still talking that shit, Amalie? Even your mother stopped that. Only a fool would pour a perfectly good beer down a hole in the earth."

"Don't listen to him, *m'ija*. He's grumpy in his old age."

But she's smiling. They are both smiling.

"I've got . . ." He looks at me. "Milk? But I could fix up some—"

Mami ignores him, and goes straight to the refrigerator, taking out all of his food and then pouring me a plastic cup of Kool-Aid. She mixes everything he's got with some water in a pot on the stove and then turns some flour into fry bread.

Grampa and I sit across from each other, both of us with our faces in our hands, our elbows on the plastic tablecloth. Only I keep lifting up my elbows to make a skin-peeling squishy sound. Grampa starts lifting his feet up and down so it makes the same rhythm on the sticky linoleum floor. I laugh before I remember I hate him. Then I look away and count the little rows of mesquite beans drying on top of the refrigerator. Mami brings the pot to the table, sets it on a folded shawl.

Grampa winks at me. He breaks up his fry bread and stuffs it in there, too, along with the potatoes and hot dogs and pickles.

Mami and I sleep together on a pile of fringed shawls on the fold-out sofa. In the half darkness, Mami turns her face to me and I see that her eyes are widening. She seems to float in and out behind them, like a person coming to a window, looking out for a moment, then disappearing. She's here, then somewhere else, then here again.

She taps my nose and says, "I have a present for you, angel."

"A secret?"

She pulls a packet of tissue from the pocket of her jeans and unwinds it carefully. A piece of a broken bracelet knotted around a silver key ring falls gently onto my pillow.

"I found it at the church dinner, behind the Dumpsters. I asked the lady who cleans there if I could have it, and she said she thought it would be okay. It's pretty, huh?"

I loop my finger through the key ring, close it tight in my hand and curl into her. Her arms are thin and bruised around me, her hand a swollen awkward shape now. A raised white scar spills down her wrist like poured milk. But her body is more relaxed. I weave my fingers through her hair, raise my chin to look at her, and trace the delicate line of her cheek where her bottom lip is beginning to tremble. I watch as it grows to a rattle, her jaw loosening.

"What?"

Her mouth steadies as she looks at me. "If God talks to people . . ." Her eyes are so wide now. "I'm trying to figure out . . . if God talks to us and we can hear him . . ."

"Probably you can ask Grampa."

"Yes, baby." Her jaw erupts again.

She pulls the blanket tighter around us and I lean into the hot web of her breathing, the warm, sooty smell of her hair.

"Mami, when are we going home?"

"Home?"

"Back to Papi."

A curtain pulls closed and her eyes are blank.

"Mami?"

But she turns away, arcs her foot back to touch mine, and goes to sleep.

In the morning, while Mami and I are at the gas station buying her cigarettes, I pull a folded street map from a shelf by the register and ask her to buy it. She looks down at me and shakes her head.

"That's not what you want."

It's a map of Fresno and she returns it to its place on the shelf.

"You got a map of the world?" she asks the clerk.

It's a teenage boy, his face pockmarked with acne, and he looks at her as if he's scared. *Scared of what?* He explains to Mami that he doesn't believe any person driving by is likely to need a map of the world.

Mami glares at him. "For fuck's sake," she mumbles. She lights one of the cigarettes and then picks out a folded map marked "USA."

At home, we sit at the kitchen table and unfold the map so that it stretches between us. Mami uses a black marker to draw a line along the folds that's straight at first, but as she considers it more, grows wrinkled and knotted, turning back on itself, intersecting and pushing on slowly until it reaches a tiny road at the intersection of highways, where she draws a bold dot to mark Grampa's house. I trace my finger along the line.

"Where are we now?"

"In Los Angeles."

"But where is Los Angeles?"

"In California."

"Where's Papi?"

"In Arizona."

"Where's Avikwaame?"

"That's enough questions, Alice." She kisses my forehead.

"But why is Papi in Arizona and why is Los Angeles in California?"

"What does it matter?" Mami says. "They're all in the world."

Grampa looks out at us from his brown easy chair in the living room, where he's in front of the television, drinking a beer.

"Because sometimes the world is all in one place," he says, "right, *nieta*?"

Mami's face is on mine, and I figure out she doesn't want me to answer.

"More likely," she says, "you're stuck in a place and the world shrinks and fits itself into it." She pulls me onto her lap and nestles her chin in my hair. "Anyway, it's not so complicated. Alice just wants to know how we got here."

"No, with or without a map, it's not complicated. It's easy to find a place, what's hard is to *be* somewhere."

"No," Mami says, "unless you are Kwikumat himself, you can never *be* anywhere."

"Phew!" Grampa wipes the sweat from his face with the back of his arm, and speaks so recklessly, he spits. "Nonsense. It's not just mountains that stand in the earth. You think you are some kind of turtle, carrying your home around on your back?"

"Yes," Mami says. She swings me up and carries me out on her back in Mamita's red shawl. "As a matter of fact, Papito, I do."

Grampa insists that Mami empty our plastic bags and I watch her pile them into corners of the room. First, she puts them in the closet: a pair of jeans, a glittery beaded tube top, a pair of my shoes that don't fit any-more. Then she sets them all up in a lopsided pyramid leaning against a big sack of mesquite beans in the kitchen. She divides our things and makes two piles. My too-small shoes stay in her pile. She just looks at the piles for a little while, then she starts to pack them into a trash bag.

"Are we going somewhere?" I ask.

She studies me, twists her mouth to the side, and then finally picks my shoes back out of the trash bag.

"Mami, *Mom!* Are we going to leave?"

She hands me my doll, a sponge doll with a missing arm and one shoe, then picks up the trash bag and walks past Grampa in the living room, out into the cemented lot nearby where there is a broken basketball hoop. From the window, I watch as she dumps the entire contents onto the chalk-strewn cement, and then gathers up crinkly newspapers and paper bags from the Dumpster nearby and buries the pile of junk in a heap of crumbled paper. Grampa tries to get out of his brown chair. He grips the arms and rocks himself forward twice before he gets enough momentum to push himself out of the chair. He grabs the TV table once he's standing, and steadies himself. "My goddamn feet," he says. He crosses through the kitchen and looks over my head, through the window at Mami. When he sees her stuffing fist-size balls of paper into the heap, he bursts out laughing. As he heads out the door, his braid swings and I can hear him giggling. I follow him into the alley, my face still wet and stinging from crying.

Mami strikes a match on the bottom of her shoe and drops it on the pile. It lights quickly, making a big cloud of smoke. The papers curl themselves into delicate black shapes with razor fingers and sharpened teeth. The fire colors and scents the air a peculiar woodsy gray. It makes a few dramatic sparks and then dies down, smoldering and sparking sporadically as if it has made up its mind to die.

Grampa goes back into the house, and returns with his hands full. He gives Mami a jar of whiskey, opens himself a bottle of beer, and drags a trash can over to the pile, tilting and rolling it over carefully on its side. Then he starts picking up clothes from the pile. The little newspaper monsters collapse softly in his hands. He piles all of our stuff into the trash can. Then he tears up more newspapers, crumples them into little balls and places them inside the can. Mami drops another match on it and Grampa fans and blows into the can.

"At home, we burned everything all the time, we'd do anything to keep warm. Your mother used to make those big *fogatas* with all the trash. You remember, Lee? And sometimes people would come over and throw in an old end table, a chest of drawers, anything to keep it going."

"What's *fogatas*?" I ask.

"I would never have thought that a daughter of mine would not know how to light a fire." He clinks his bottle against Mami's jar, then catches me as I run by.

"Get those bags and sticks, *nieta*. You have to keep feeding it. Only dead stuff, nothing soft or wet. Fires like them crispy and dried up."

As I walk around the vacant lot collecting sticks and papers, the light changes to a soft blue-gray. From the trash can, the fire blinks and spits. Mami's face is lit orange. She leans against Grampa, drinking her whiskey.

"Well, I guess this is unpacking," Grampa laughs a strange long squeak of a laugh. It seems like he finds it so funny he can barely get the laugh out of his mouth.

"Hell, yeah," Mami laughs with him.

"It's like at home," Grampa says, "just like at home."

"Like what?" I shout. "What home? What! Is! *Fogatas!*"

I can't believe what Grampa has said. He doesn't know home, he's never even been with us before.

He says, "Like this, little one. Bonfires burning up all of our trash and everyone three sheets to the wind and your little mami running around looking just like you, asking the same silly questions."

Mami smiles. "She's an angel."

"What's that story Carmen used to tell you all the time?"

Mami lifts me up so I can look into the fire. "When I was a little girl," she says. "I met a condor and he said to me, 'Do you want meat?' He promised me meat so I stepped out of my mother's house and he grabbed me up in his talons and flew off with me. We went all the way up to the ears of the mountain, and he hid me in his cave."

Mami shifts me onto her hip. It's dark now. The fire throws sparks and I peek at them out of one eye, the other squeezed tight. I look down into the trash can and up at the stars, up, down, up, down. The night whirls. It's all light and fire and Mami's story.

"The grasshopper," Grampa hiccups.

"Yes," Mami says. "A grasshopper took me home to my grand-

84

mother who hid me in a barrel. But the condor found me. He scratched and scratched with his beak and his talons to get at me till finally he tired and flew away."

Mami puts me down and I run as fast as I can around the lot. The condor flies all around us. His wings are so big and black they blot out the stars. I kick him, grab his wing, *Get! Shoo!* I tell him.

I fight and run.

Grampa and Mami are laughing.

I stand still, make my face mean. I tug on Mami's jeans. "Don't tell this part!" I say.

But they're ignoring me. "And when my grandmother opened the barrel . . ." Mami says.

Grampa giggles, finishing for her. "She found only dry bones!" He grabs the rim of the trash can and leans on it, his words slurred. "What the *hell* does that mean?"

I push Mami, kick her foot, and fold my arms in front of me. "You weren't supposed to say that part," I pout.

But now Mami is laughing, too. She picks me up again and strokes my hair. Then she shifts me onto her hip and lets me take a drink from the jar. The whiskey burns my throat, makes my eyes water. It tastes horrible. Mami and Grampa laugh at me. They laugh and laugh.

TEN

Mami is making me a jingle dress for powwow, and sewing more beads onto Mamita's turtle shawl for herself. We lay on the floor together next to Grampa's easy chair, with the sewing machine between us.

"Your grandma made this for my first haircut." She pulls the beads through the shawl awkwardly, holding it close to her face. "Mamita taught me how to weave," she says, "but not how to sew beads. What do you think?"

She holds it up for us. The beads are so loose around the turtle pattern that Grampa says, "That turtle's grown hair."

"Hairy turtle shawl," Mami says. "Soon to be very famous."

I peek through the sewing machine. "Why don't we go home?" I ask her.

Mami looks at me. "What home?"

"Papi and school."

"Because if we did, it wouldn't be home anymore."

"Why not?"

"You'll see, baby. You're getting older."

She slips the red-and-white box dress over my head and all the little metal cones clang in unison around me. I jump around the room, hop, hop, making jingles everywhere, clang into the kitchen, clang into the living room, clang rapturously around Grampa's easy chair.

When Mami's turtle shawl is finished, she lets me try it on. I crawl around the living room, poking my head in and out from under the shawl, pretending to be a turtle.

The flyer from the American Indian Center says "Grand Entry at Noon," but we're not ready to leave until after dinner. "Aren't we late?" I ask Mami.

"Naah," she laughs. "They'll start on Indian time, that's about now." Grampa doesn't get up, but looks us over from his easy chair.

"You're not coming?" I ask him.

"Grampa only wants to be an Indian when it's convenient," Mami says.

He ignores her, switching the TV on, and turning up the volume.

When we get to the powwow, it's already dark out, but people are still arriving, lining up halfheartedly outside a high school gymnasium.

Inside, an announcer speaks from a podium underneath a basketball hoop. "It's about twelve o'clock powwow standard time. Are we ready yet?" He looks over the line, where no one is listening to him. "Almost?" he says. "Not quite? Okay." He looks out at every-one in the bleachers and says resignedly, "You know this is why we lost the Indian wars."

And then it begins, spiraling around the plastic lines on the floor of the basketball court: birds like in the stories, a man covered in glossy black feathers, crows and owls, and all of them dancing around the gym, and some of them seem to be flying. When I close my eyes, I hear the movement of the drum circles competing, the sound of howling voices, of wind, of birds in flight, of late-night sirens and crackling fires, and I hear the jingle of the other girls' dresses around me. Clang! Clang! The drum circle calling, How-ool! Where will these birds fly? Out through the metal-framed windows, into the street and around all the houses, swooping into kitchens and around TVs, faster than cars. And what about Grampa? We'll swoop around his easy chair, too.

I'll fly condor wings, and when I get there I'll ride around him in circles. And then I'll scoop him up with my talons and we will ride my wings back to Papi. What kind of bird is Papi? Maybe he is not a bird, but a coyote. And Abel? Abel is a mountain lion proba-bly, like Mami, but no, Mami is not a lion now. She is a butterfly. Look at her sail, wings fluttering up and down, her face peeking out of the shawl as she jumps. Float! Fly! I look at my moccasins: *Two Feet Jump!*

An older butterfly-woman takes my hand and pulls me off the basketball court when they call for the Fancy Shawl Dancers. She stills me with her hand on my shoulder when the drum begins.

A big man sits on the bleachers next to me. Behind him, an identical little boy tugs hard on the man's braid until the man grabs it at the nape of his neck. Then they start a tug of war, each pulling one end.

Mami is the only fancy dancer. "Stiff competition here today," the announcer laughs, but after Mami's red shawl answers the drums in the most amazing S-shaped flight, he almost whispers into the microphone, "True, folks, she's the only one out there, but hell, the woman can fly!"

At the Indian Health Services table, a bunch of nurses try to get Mami to sign a petition for a new Indian clinic in the city. One of the nurses tugs me close to her while Mami listens to her read the survey.

What is the primary impediment to your access to health care? Check One:

No job?

No money?

No car?

Another nurse lifts my dress to look closer at all the red spots. "Fungus," she says, crinkling her nose. "Ringworm, probably. How long has this child been like this?"

But the nurse who's reading seems to know Mami. She looks

over Mami's shoulder, points out where she hasn't checked a box.

The nurse lets my dress down, goes over to some man eating fry bread. Little specks of white sugar freckle his chin. She comes back with a slip of paper he's peeled from his pad.

"You've got to get this filled." She hands it to Mami. "Put it on her twice a day. What has she been doing to get like that?"

The other nurse takes the survey back from Mami and stands between them.

"They're chicken pox," I tell her, but Mami stares at the marble pattern on the hallway floor.

"Right? Right, Mami?"

But she doesn't answer. The nurse tries to smile at us, but Mami pulls me away.

We don't get home till very late and we fall asleep on the sofa without even unfolding it, wrapped up in Mami's Hairy Turtle Shawl. Sometime in the bluest part of the night, Mami shakes me awake. She curls her fingers around my nightgown. "Listen, she says. "I want to tell you something important. It's these twins, they're in my head. I can feel them poking around, looking through my eyes. Here!" She shoves something into my chest, sticks tied together and wound with juncus leaves and slices of bread.

"Bury it," she says. "Bury it! Make them go away."

"Mami?"

"Go, go do it!"

She gathers me into her chest. "*Pequeñita, oh,* you're just a baby," she laughs, strokes my hair into a plait behind my ears. She seems to be falling asleep, but whispers softly, crying, "Angel, the leaves said you are the only one I can have. All those voices crowded into my head, they're all the other ones packed into me, all the babies I couldn't have."

"What leaves?"

"The leaves. Mamita read them. Three little whole ones scattered away, and then there was you, the torn one. Mamita bit it before she threw them. 'This is Alice,' she said, and then we knew."

I think about my doll, the broken doll we dug up on the reservation. Were her pieces missing before or after she was lost?

Mami stands. She paces for a bit and then goes to the window. "Let's go for a walk," she says. I wrap my arms around her neck and ride piggyback out into the living room. It's quiet but for the sounds outside: cars going by, distant sirens. Down the hill and off to the bottom of the block past the gas station. I lean into Mami's shoulder and inhale the smell of her. It's different now. She doesn't wash her hair, which has grown out. It knots up and breaks, catching around her breasts and beneath her armpits.

I fall asleep on her shoulder and when I wake up again, the world has divided itself into two colors: a pale blue and a ragged-edged pink sky. The sun is coming.

"What does the sun do at night?" I ask her.

"Guides the movements of the dead," she says softly.

We buy a cup of coffee at the gas station and then go home. I stand on a chair while she cooks. She moves so quickly around the kitchen, sipping her coffee and assembling pancakes.

I point to the pan she's heating on the stove. "Don't put your hands in there," I say.

"Of course not, angel." She pours batter into the pan and waits by the stove. Her hips are visible above her low-slung jeans. She wears a sparkly tube top. She looks so pretty, smiling at me. When she flips the pancake, it misses the pan, and falls to the floor. We're giggling as we clean the split pancake off the floor. I sit at the table with the two halves of a pancake she has reunited on the plate for me. Grampa has so much food. He gets a big box every month from Indian Health. Mami sits with me for just a second, but then she's up again, pacing and worrying her cigarette.

"You and me have got lion souls, baby doll."

"I know." My pancake is too hot, so I hold the fork with two hands and blow on it.

"Grampa says my dreams don't mean nothing. Do you think that's true?"

But I'm chewing. It tastes like floor cleaner.

"You know I had a dream once and my grandmother had the same dream. Can you believe that? I was a lion. I was wild!"

She roars and pounces across the table, and it makes me giggle into my hands. I get down on the floor and admire my yellow-gold fur, so soft, and my fuzzy orange tail with its fine hairs like thread. I wave it up and down sleepily and then rest my paws on the edge of the table.

"I was ferocious," Mami says, "and in my grandmother's dream, she couldn't settle me. *'Tranquilla, tranquillaté,'* she was always saying, but I didn't have it in me to rest. My grandmother was a good woman, angel, and so was yours. She never let me down, never once, and feeding a lion is not easy."

She gets a sponge out of the closet and fills a bucket with soapy water, then runs the soapy sponge across the kitchen windows. As she moves around, she sings to herself and dances, using a spoon as a microphone. When she's done with the windows, she scrubs the stove, washes the dishes, dries them, takes out all the canned goods and wipes down the cabinets. I feel full and drowsy after eating. I can't keep my head up.

When I wake, the morning light is a bright triangle in the kitchen. The schoolkids on the corner are cawing like scared-up crows. My fork is stuck under a thin film of syrup on my paper plate. Mami is on the kitchen floor, scrubbing with a tiny brush—a toothbrush—at no discernible spot. Grampa has come to the kitchen doorway, his hair sprouting in little flyaways from his braid. He looks at my undershirt and flowered panties, streaked with fine lines of red and orange from where my nose bled and I spilled orange soda. Then he picks me up from the table, carries me out to the sofabed, and tucks me in. When I wake in the late afternoon, damp strands of my hair sticking to my face, Grampa is still in his easy chair staring at me.

I feel dizzy and cold at breakfast, my coffee and tortillas turning in my stomach. Grampa takes my temperature, and goes in to try to wake Mami where she sleeps on the couch. But she won't stir. He shakes her, leans close to her and feels her forehead.

"Get up, Lee," he says. "What's wrong with you, honey? This baby is sick."

But she doesn't move. She sleeps for two whole days, and when Grampa and I wake up on the third day, she's gone. She doesn't come back all day.

When the sun goes down, Grampa tucks me into his easy chair with a blanket and tells me to sit tight while he goes to the pharmacy. I'm erecting a fort with the cushions from the easy chair when I hear a dull tap on the living room window. I pull the window up and lean out. It's Mami in a woolen stocking cap. "My angel," she says. "Open the door, *m'ija.*"

We hug and the scent of her rushes around me: a mixture of body odor and fetid street smells.

"Grampa's at the pharmacy," I say. "I think he's mad at you."

She pulls her hat off and I see that her hair is shaved again. The bristles cover her head like a mist of ashes. She points her foot out in front of her. "Isn't it pretty, angel?" A black wire snakes around her ankle and climbs up her leg. "I saw it on the street and I asked this lady if I could have it and she said she thought that it would be okay."

"It's pretty," I say. But the dirty wire is rusty and biting into her skin, making little red indentations and blood spots. "We should wash it," I say. "How come you slept so long?"

"Angel, your cheeks are all red." She puts her palm on my forehead. "You're hot."

"I have a temperature," I say. "Where have you been?"

"Oh, everywhere," she says. "Just forgot my shoes."

I smile.

While she's in the bathroom, I take slices of bread, potato chips, all sorts of cheese, and pickles and pile it all onto a plate. I make a huge sandwich and set it at the table with a glass of milk. As I sort through her plastic bags, I realize they are almost empty. There are no clothes, no maps. Only my old shoes. The laces are rotted and the shoes feel wet, but tucked inside are plastic bags filled with pictures: my faded ID card from the school lunch program at the reservation, a beaded dragonfly I used to wear in my braids, wound strands of my hair.

Two days later, Mami piles everything we have left into plastic bags and leans them up against the front door.

Grampa blocks the kitchen doorway. "I promised Al a snowball," he says. "Wouldn't you like a snowball, *muñeca*?"

"There's no time, angel," Mami says.

Grampa makes a surprised face. "No time for a snowball?"

He keeps looking at the clock hanging above the stove. He rubs his face with the whole of his palm, up and down, up and down, covering his eyes. He won't look at Mami, doesn't even look at me.

"What's wrong?" Mami says finally.

"Never mind. Get on outta here." Grampa takes his hat off. "Go ahead, quick."

"My snowball!" I say. "Mami, plea-ese!"

She laughs a little, squints at Grampa, "Okay, angel, go ahead, then."

I take the dollar from Grampa and run into the living room. I can't find my sandals so I slip on Mami's flip-flops. They stretch out past my heels in long strips of green foam. Then I run, as fast as I can, down the hill to the gas station.

I eat the chocolate snowball slowly, walking home, until, at the top of the hill, I make out two police cars parked at angles in the street. Mami stands barefoot (I have her shoes!), shouting at one of the officers. She makes a windmill of her arms, cursing and shouting at them. Then she puts her head down and walks calmly toward the car.

. . .

I run, gravity against me, up the hill. I drop the snowball and I feel the cold juice seeping through my shirt. When I get to the police car between the street and the curb, Grampa scoops me up high on his hip. But the cars are pulling away. I lean into him, stare down into the paper bag he cradles in his other arm.

Inside, I stand in the middle of the living room, trying to figure out what to do. A colorful six-pack inside a paper bag sits on the coffee table: amber-colored bottles with tiny beads of sweat around their necks. Grampa sits down on the sofa, uncaps a beer and drinks hard. I run into the kitchen. My face is slick and I try to slow down my breathing, so I can see through the tears. I get a chair and pull the phone book from the top of the refrigerator. It comes down heavy and quick, and makes a thud on the kitchen floor as it slips from my hands. I kneel down on the floor in front of it and flip through the pages quickly. Grampa comes to the kitchen doorway.

"Help me!" I shout. "Help me find the number for the police!"

"Settle down, Alice."

"But I'm trying to find—"

"Stop it!" he yells. "Stop it, child!"

I freeze and Grampa goes away into the living room. I rest my forehead on the phone book and cry.

. . .

When I wake up, I'm alone in Grampa's bed with Mamita's turtle shawl pulled up around me. I get up and go out the back door, climb over the concrete fence and out into the alley. The shawl picks up trash and drags plastic bags and smashed-up newspapers behind me. I call for my condor wings, close my eyes and listen for the bird approaching. But he won't come. I look around me for which way to go, pick a rubber ball that's been cut in half out of the trash and throw it against a concrete fence. Then I see Grampa coming toward me. I pick up the ball again and throw it at him. He comes closer and I hit him with my fists. I hit him and kick him as hard as I can, over and over until I fall to the ground and a broken bottle slices my ankle. I break loose like a window hit with a bat, and shake wildly on the ground.

Grampa picks me up; he wraps the shawl around me, gathers it together in front of me and lifts my hand up to hold it. We walk together, me hiccuping and sobbing and Grampa silent, until we get to the gas station where he buys me a Coke. At home, I sit in his lap with iodine on my ankle. He rocks me and blows softly on the cut where it stings from the iodine. His fingers tap my back softly, drumming out a steady rhythm powerful enough to make me forget.

ELEVEN

Mami has been gone for four days. Whenever I ask Grampa about it, he puts me to work. For example: "Is Mami coming back?"

"Of course, *flaquita*. Is that what you're sitting around waiting for? Pick up all those crayons if you're anxious."

"It's not true she went with them for cigarettes."

"Maybe they were out. Maybe she had to try somewhere else. Maybe these clothes will get folded if we stare at them long enough."

Whenever I ask too many questions, he puts me in the bathtub. I turn over in the water and flatten my hands against the porcelain. Pushing against the bottom of the tub, I drown the twins; hold them down until they stop hanging on her, and float away, pale blue and lifeless. *When I get to the surface, when I can't hold my breath anymore, she'll be home.* I flip over, so that my face breaks the water, and listen for her. "Kumastamxo," I whisper. "Kumastamxo."

When Grampa walks by the open door I splash in the water and shout at him, "Kumastamxo!" He stops moving, stares for a moment at the broken earring and key chain I've arranged on the sink, and finally answers me. He sits on the edge of the tub, fishes out the washcloth and attacks my ears.

"She's sick, *m'ija*. Homesick maybe."

I hold on to his arm and his hand stills against my cheek.

"Did they take her home to Papi?"

"The home you are always crying about?" He scrubs the back of my neck. "How do you always get so filthy?" He lifts my hands and examines the fine arcs of mud under the nails.

"Maybe she needs some other home, some home she can't get to. I'm old, Al. I don't know much anymore."

I start to cry. I don't know where it comes from, but it rattles me from the inside like all the sticks in the circle hitting the drum at once. He pulls me out in a towel and we sit together on the toilet seat.

"I'll tell you what Carmen used to say. A long time ago, the priests came and told your grandma and her friends all about heaven. But nobody was interested. Indians wanted to stay on the mountain forever. And look at you and me, you and your mami— all these hundreds of miles away from anywhere we ought to be. Baby, if you dig your feet under the linoleum like that you're just going to get filthy again."

But I'm trying to dig, to plant myself like a tree, to root.

• • •

Every day I bury a matchstick in the dirt, from a box I have stolen from Grampa's kitchen drawer. Today is number six. I plant it by the rat hole in the fence, and then draw a map in the newsprint TV guide Grampa has given me for coloring. A blue crayon line goes straight, loops around the broken TV sitting in the yard, up over the clothesline, twice around the drainpipe, and in through the living room window where I sleep. I keep the book tucked under the couch, and only take it out when he's drunk or sleeping.

Grampa's feet are covered in blisters, small red spots and wide leaf-shaped marks. They burrow between his toes and wind around his ankles. Every day they grow angrier. At first he just ignores them, but after the nurse at the free clinic downtown tells him they're important, he makes me check them every day. I lift them up, move them around in the light of the TV static and report, "Yep, they're still there, Grampa." He breathes in deep then, and starts working his Stetson on and off, rubbing his head, putting it on, taking it off. We make a poultice by boiling tree sap and mesquite beans, crush them between two sheets of wax paper with a soup pan and mat them with Vaseline to his feet.

I've buried my ninth matchstick when he limps out of the truck wincing, "That's it!" and we get back into the pickup and go downtown to talk to the nurse.

"It's pretty bad," she tells him. "Ray, you need to be on dialysis. The Doc says the facility—"

"I ain't moving," he says. "No way, Arlie, tell them I said fuck that." He grabs my hand and we go back home, but Arlie calls on the phone.

"Like I told you before," he says, "I ain't moving."

A long pause, "Well then, I'll die here."

He looks over at me. I sit in the halo of the TV, my hair wet, my knees folded up inside the tent of his red flannel shirt. He turns then, faces the kitchen, and lowers his voice.

"Right," he says. "All right. No, she's got her mother. I ain't pig-headed, Arlie, just not stupid anymore."

"Let them all try!" he says to the ringing phone two days later. "I ain't moving. Hell if I'm falling for this SSI bullshit again."

Then a car radio sails through the front window, crashing just where I lay on my stomach seconds before, drawing a new map onto the pages of my TV guide. We stand there together, listening to the breeze flicking the blinds against the glass-speckled windowsill. It seems louder than the raucous shattering that came minutes before. Grampa picks up the car stereo, a big black rusted thing that leaves pieces of shrapnel on my map, and hauls it out into the middle of the street.

"Fuck you, you little shits, we ain't goin' nowhere!"

Some people come out of their screen doors to watch the rusty old Nova drive slowly down the street, full of teenage boys hissing at the girls carrying groceries and pushing strollers on the sidewalk. The radio in their car makes a repetitive vibration that shimmies through the house. One of the boys holds his hand out of the window and says "How" to Grampa. They all fall apart in laughter, rocking back and forth like they have to pee, and are trying to keep themselves from doing it.

I help stretch the gray duct tape across the window, fastening a big piece of clear plastic. I look at all the wrinkles in his face. He is probably two hundred.

"This is a *real* house, right, Grampa?"

"Yes."

"Fuck them!" I say. "We ain't goin' nowhere!"

"Oh shit," Grampa laughs. "Don't say that, honey."

We have to sign in at a gate in order to see her. Grampa talks to the doctor, and I approach Mami where she is slumped over a conference table. One arm is stretched out, wrapped around a cup filled with cigarette butts and ashy gray water. A cigarette, burned down to her knuckles, is between her first two fingers. Her forehead is pressed onto the paper tablecloth. Her other arm hangs limp at her side. She gasps a little now and then, choking on her sobs. Her hair is matted into tiny little dirty knots. She smells of cigarettes and vomit.

When I tug on her shoulders, she moves like a dead body, slamming against the back of the chair, her head flung backward. Long lines of tears are driving clean highways down her dirty face. She won't move when I tug on her arms from the front, so I get behind her and push her shoulders forward until she stumbles up to her feet. I push her to the common room and we sit on a vinyl couch.

"I brought your mami's turtle shawl," I say. I wrap it around her, tucking it in at the collar of her blue hospital gown so it will stay around her. She stares straight ahead. I crawl onto her lap and sit sideways, my legs stretched across her thighs. I wrap my arms around her neck and lean into her chest but her arms stay at her sides, her eyes empty. I try to make her hold me, but I can't lift her arms, they are dead heavy.

We sit there for a long time and I pretend, "Good night, angel" and "Sleep tight" and "Don't let the bedbugs bite."

I tell her about my map, about the crash through the window. I tell her that I have brought her shoes, and I ask if she wants to come home with us. But she doesn't move or speak or anything.

Finally, her eyes stir and she gets up. I fall off her lap when she stands, but she doesn't seem to notice me. The shawl has fallen, half on my knees, half on the floor. She walks away into the hallway, and Grampa finally stops talking to the doctor and takes my hand. His feet hurt him so badly now that he has to use a cane, and I look into the hallway to see if Mami has noticed this, but she shuffles away. When the gate makes a loud sound opening, a long buzz, she turns around, her mouth curving slightly up into a smile, and steps toward us just as it closes.

• • •

Twelve matchsticks, and I've decided to dig them up and light them. I flip through the pages of my TV guide, but my maps are all unreliable, mountains and blobs and shapes that lead me nowhere, so I just dig around everywhere I can remember until I've found seven of them. I sit down cross-legged in the alley and light each one on the ragged cement. The sulfur crawls up my nose into the space between the back of my eyes and my forehead. I watch the blue-yellow light, so many colors dancing around inside it, until it burns down to an inky black softness and I have to drop it. I try to hold each one longer and longer, until a faint gray-black shadow appears on my fingertips.

Afterward I scrape up all the ashes and stubs of sticks and bury them far away from Grampa's house where some men have come to repair the sidewalk. He calls to me from where he leans out of the screen door, his cowboy hat hiding half his face in shadow.

"Get back here, Alice," he says. "I told you not to wander too far."

I scrape an X on the wet cement with the heel of my shoe and run back to Grampa's house.

On our next visit, Mami is in a better mood. She has piled on clothes from the Goodwill donations, six or seven skirts at once. And she has made two messy braids out of her knotted hair and tied them together at the ends. She squats by the TV, where she talks to a huge man whose stubby legs are stuffed into tan pants.

"Where will we die?" she asks him. "They've left us nowhere to die."

He just rubs his hands up and down his thighs.

"This tells where I come from." She shows him the shawl she's recovered, then extends her hand as if meeting him for the first time. She leans in and whispers confidentially, "They think my name is Amalie, but it's Carmen, Carmen. See, this tells where we come from.

"There's my angel." She sees me behind the chair I hold, calls me to her and hugs me hard.

"This is my baby. She's come to get me out of here.

"You want a beer?" she asks him suddenly.

He doesn't answer.

"Yeah, me too, but that ain't right. I want to be a saint someday. Like Jesus, like God, like Kwikumat," she laughs. "Beer and cigarettes are for feeding the devil."

In her room she shows me a devil she's made from papiermâché. Around it are all sorts of offerings: Hershey's Kisses and paper cups, and in its mouth, a limp cigarette, burned down to the filter.

"I'm going to escape," she tells me in the bathroom. "I don't belong here."

She lifts me up to the sink so I can wash my hands, and as she rubs the bar of soap into my open palms, I can see shoes peeking out of one of the stalls, and legs in pantyhose. A wicked witch squashed under a house. Just when I expect her feet to curl up, the toilet flushes and I see the rest of her, a woman humming to herself as she lies on the floor, flushing the toilet over and over.

At Grampa's house I'm punished and have to stay inside.

"It's just a TV," I've been yelling at my sponge doll, "can't you tell the difference between a TV and a monster?" I throw her at the TV. "It's just a TV!"

Grampa tells me to pick her up, that we'll fix her or get a new one. "I don't want her," I say. "I don't want a new one, either. It's just a doll, you're not supposed to really love it like a person." Grampa looks me up and down slowly.

I roll my eyes. *"Can't you tell the difference between a doll and a baby!"*

As I stare through the plastic on the front window, I wonder if Mami will escape and come walking down the street.

It's lunchtime at the hospital the next time we visit. We sit at a table with Mami and her two friends. Albert, who keeps putting his fork down and standing up at the table to shimmy his arms and shake his hips between bites. He sticks his tongue out like he's taunting someone, then sits down and scoops up another spoonful of collard greens. Her other friend is pregnant, and missing two front

109

teeth. We eat at a concrete picnic table with benches attached to it.

"It's chicken fried steak," Grampa says, when he notices me pushing the meat around on my pastel-green tray. The small steak has an oily white covering of congealed gravy and it sits atop a lump of serrated carrots. The brown sugar on top of the carrots makes them look like the surface of an emery board. I pick one up with my fingers and try to file my nails with it, but Grampa smacks my hand.

Everyone chews sullenly.

"It ain't bad, Lee," Grampa says. "It just all tastes the same."

"It *is* the same," Albert says. "They just disguise it to look like different types of food. They're with the FBI, you know."

"What's the FBI?"

"Shhh," Albert warns.

I lay my head on my arm, stretched out on the table, and yawn. I just want to go home. I ask Mami, "Why don't you eat with us at home?"

Grampa interrupts, "She'll be home soon."

I look at Mami, sitting up straight for her and ignoring Grampa. "Can I spend the night with you?"

"You don't want to stay here," Mami says. She looks tired, too.

"Grampa's too old to look after me."

Grampa glares at me. "Who you calling old, you little shrimp?"

I climb off the bench and go to the window. We're high up, but the window has a tic-tac-toe of metal grates attached to it. Outside, the hospital looks like a park, with a fountain in the middle big enough for people. I wonder if they swim in it when we're not around. Everything looks green outside, green and yellow. This is when I get the idea for the bread baby.

"What do you need it for?" Grampa asks, when I try to go out the back door with a bag of bread.

"I'm hungry."

"Baby, I'm not gonna have you burying food. I ain't gonna have any of that nonsense."

I scream, a choking wail that surprises me, and then I can't stop crying. "Please," I beg. "Please?"

"What for, *flaca*?" His voice is soft. "Tell me."

"To make her better."

"Honey, she ain't gonna be better if we bury this bread."

"Why not?"

" 'Cause as much as we want it to be, it ain't that simple. We can't solve everything the old ways. We got bigger problems now and all kinds of new medicine to take care of this stuff."

"They don't know about this."

"You got to be so stubborn?"

"Can we bring her home, Grampa? Please?"

"Soon, soon, baby. You think I'm too old, don't you?"

"No." Yes, but I feel bad for saying so.

"Well, you're right, what you need is your mami, and she's gonna come home soon and you won't have to live with an old Indian who's too sick to look after you, eh?"

. . .

When we get to the hospital this time, something's different. She's Mami all the same, but she looks so skinny and fragile. Her eyes are swollen, rimmed in deep red, and she's quiet. She holds me in her lap and we play and talk to each other.

"She's just speaking nonsense," the doctor says to Grampa. The nurses tell us she just says it over and over, *Machu Wayra, Machu Wayra*.

Grampa stands up quickly. "Ancestor sickness," he tells them curtly. "That means ancestor sickness." He studies Mami. "How do I get her out of here?"

"We think she should stay."

"I signed her in," he yells suddenly. "Why can't I sign her out?"

But it's almost a week before we can take her home and Grampa's not supposed to be driving anymore. On the way to the hospital, a policeman gave him a ticket for pulling too slowly from the sidewalk into traffic, "with no regard," he said, "for anybody else on the street." He took away his license and drove us home. But we just took a bus back that night and got the truck.

"I'm going in, Al, but your mami's coming out."

"To jail?" On his television, when people are "goin' in" they mean to jail.

"No, baby, although it might as well be. To the Home."

"The Home," I test the word out loud. I imagine the house that Ms. Ida drew for me back in the shelter. A long, long driveway and rows and rows of flowers.

"Not any kind of home, though," he says. "Really."

" 'Cause when you get there," I ask, "it won't be home anymore?"

"Yeah, something like that."

As soon as we leave the hospital, Mami starts singing. When Grampa tries to talk to her, she just sings. When we go to bed, she lies next to me and draws shapes on my back with her finger while she sings. She's already in the shower singing when I wake in the morning. It's not a pretty song. It's sad. Grampa mixes sugar into milk for me and then pours some of his coffee into my mug and we have coffee together and listen to her sing.

When we're finished, I stand on a chair and help Grampa wash out the mugs.

"Why is Mami mad at you, Grampa?"

"What makes you think she's mad at me?"

"Is it because you let the police take her?"

"It's complicated, Alice."

"But you always say that."

"I don't know. I guess she thinks I ain't Indian no more." He stuffs the dish towel in the drawer and slams it. "Aw, hell, it's the twentieth century, ain't it? It's not like I could just go on being an Indian."

TWELVE

Grampa says he's driving himself to The Home. Arlie sits at the kitchen table with her hands folded up in front of her. "That's ridiculous," she says. "We'll send an ambulance."

"If I'm gonna let someone else wipe my ass for the rest of my life, I'm at least driving myself there."

"You know you're a fool, Ray Black Bird? You are a foolish old man."

"Black," Grampa says. "Ray *Black*, how many times do I got to tell you that?"

"I don't listen to the foolish."

Arlie goes out the front door, letting it slam behind her, and Mami follows. I press my face up against the screen door and listen.

"It's acute," she says, "he's dying, Lee." She takes the cigarette from Mami's mouth and stomps it out.

Mami watches as the cigarette rolls under Arlie's white hospital

115

shoes, leaving smudges of ash, like pencil marks, on the concrete. Then she takes another out of the pack and lights it up. "He should stay home." She blows smoke through her shaking lips. But when she looks at Arlie, she steadies her jaw. "Shouldn't he stay home if he's dying?"

"Lee, hon, you can't take care of him. He needs things—equipment, regular medicine, professional help."

I tug on Mami's cut-off jeans and she looks down at me and rests her hand on my head.

"And you, Al, let's take a look at that fungus."

Mami sits down on the steps and smokes her cigarette while Arlie stretches out my arms.

"You know what he was eating this morning? Bacon! A man with diabetes eating bacon all wrapped up in fry bread."

"I can hear you," Grampa calls.

He goes into the backyard, where he's been fixing Mami's old bike for me. It's upside down.

"Hand me that wrench," he says, when I come through the back door.

"Are you dying, Grampa?"

His mouth becomes a tight line, a stitch across a piece of ruddy leather. "I'm going off by my lonesome," he leans down and takes my cheeks in his palms, "and I'll meet up with you two later."

"Come with us."

"I can't."

"Then we'll come with you."

"Look, *flaca*," he spins the rusty old bike wheel, and then stops it quick with his hand. He spits and makes a mark on both tires, blacker than the dusty black that it is already. "See this." He spins it slowly and brings the spots back around to meet each other. "It wheels around, and there it is again. I'll turn away for a while, but it won't be the last we see of each other."

We are all wheels? Spinning away from each other!

I put my hands on his cheeks. *"No!"* I turn his head back and forth. "No, Grampa, none of us are turning away!"

He laughs. "Oh, *flaca,* you little runt, what are we gonna do with you?"

The night before he goes to The Home, I crawl next to his chair and put my hand on his back, waiting for his breath to stop.

Breathe, I whisper. *Breathe.*

He shoots up like a released arrow asking, "Amalie? Amalie?" as if he's looking for her, but his eyes are still closed.

Mami tilts his hat down over his eyes and he goes back to sleep.

I sit between them in the cab of the truck, my knees draped onto Mami's lap so Grampa can reach the gearshift.

Outside The Home, Grampa stops the pickup.

"Well," he says, "I guess this is it."

Mami sings softly, and Grampa looks hurt.

"I thought it was the only way, Lee, but I know now . . ."

"The board is going to have to deliberate," she says very seriously.

"And I. It's just . . . I know now that I traded the only thing I had."

She stops singing, starts very softly to cry. "What are we going to do with you, young miss? Put you in ice water?"

He adjusts and readjusts the mirrors, keeps doing it over and over. Then he opens his hands, palms up, and lays them on his thighs, staring at them as if he had just been holding something and he can't figure out where it has suddenly gone. He says, "I can't give you what I've already given away."

"It's good for you," she coos, "don't cry, pretty girl, it's okay, it's okay."

Grampa begins to sob, big dry heaves as he looks away out the window. But they show in his body; his chest rocks, his hands press hard against the steering wheel.

Mami smiles, sings right into my ear as she kisses my temple, "You. You. *'I get down on my knees for you-oo.'*"

THIRTEEN

Living in Grampa's house without him is strange. Mami gives almost everything away to the Salvation Army. We take everything there in trash bags and then scrub the walls with sponges and ammonia. "We have to do it," Mami says. "They say we have to do it, Alice. We have to give everything away." She makes a big pot of soup, a watery bean soup, and just when we are about to eat it, she pours it all into the kitchen sink, smooshing it down the drain with the toilet brush.

"It was poison," she says, "they were trying to poison you."

"But I'm hungry," I whine. I haven't eaten since the night before. She takes me to the gas station and buys me a candy bar, but up in her arms, as we cross the two concrete islands, my stomach turns, and I throw it up, vomiting it onto the front of her bathrobe.

"Don't cry," Mami says. "Shhh, baby, *don't.*" And I try not to. At home I climb onto the counter to get to the jars left on top of the refrigerator and make myself a sandwich of ketchup and mustard while she rocks in Grampa's rocking chair. She stays there all day, just staring at the wall. I have to call her name over and over before she sees me and takes the sandwich I've made her.

"Oh," she says, "thank you, angel." Sometimes she pulls me into her lap, and I rock with her in the quiet, wondering what she sees that I can't make out. Grampa calls on the phone, and asks me if I'm taking care of her.

"Yeah," I answer. "Do you want to talk to her?" But Mami won't take the phone. "She's afraid of the phone," I tell Grampa.

"What's that, *flaca*?"

"She won't get on the phone."

"Oh, are you taking care of Mami, *flaca*?"

"Yes, Grampa."

"Let me talk to her."

"She's afraid of the phone."

"What's that?"

"She won't get up."

"Oh," Grampa says. "You be good now, Lee."

"I'm Alice."

"Yes. You be a good girl."

"Okay." I hang up the phone and crawl back into the chair with Mami. "Grampa says hi," I tell her. "It's okay if you're afraid of the phone." I tuck the hair behind her ears. "Don't worry, okay? I'll answer it." I lean my head into her neck, and try to sleep.

When we wake in the morning, Mami is clear-eyed and determined.

"You know what we have to do, angel?"

"What?"

"We have to take everything in there with us. We'll get away from them."

"Take everything where?"

"Into the living room." She leans against the living room doorway. "It'll be safe in there."

She's wearing jeans, a flannel shirt, and one of Grampa's sweaters. The tails are pulled out, and the collar tucked in on only one side. Over this, she wears her nubby bathrobe. Her hair is matted and oily. I haven't had to take a bath, either. Though last night I put toothpaste on both of our toothbrushes and brought one to Mami.

I help her drag things into the living room. Everything in the house goes into the living room. The bare mattress carted from Grampa's bed, the canned goods from the kitchen closet, the remaining clothes and the chest of old beaded shawls. We sleep in there, too, on the bare mattress under the turtle shawl. It gets stained with the sweat from our bodies so that curly outlines appear along the springs trying to push through. Mami tucks the hair behind my ears at night, her face close to mine. "Sweet angel," she says. "Let's pray together." *Dear God, please help us to be saints, make the voices go away.*

I feel so hot all the time with the heat turned up, so I just wear my underwear. I bury all of my other clothes in the stack of shawls and jeans piled against the front door. Still, my hair sticks to my neck and sweat collects above my lip in little droplets that taste sweet and salty. I try to poke my head out of the back door for cool air, but Mami locks it up.

"Don't go out," she says, "they'll get you if you go out."

Mostly I watch cartoons and draw maps while she sleeps, or I dance with the fancy shawls from Grampa's chest, while she just stares. She has taped all sorts of things onto the wall, mostly pictures of us that she found in Grampa's dressers. One shows Mamita, Grampa, and Mami. They stand in front of a small trailer, holding hands. Grampa is in an army uniform; his hair cut short, his eyes hidden and shy. Mamita is fat and smiling, with two braids and a ribbon dress, and Mami is a naked baby in a washtub, cupping water in her palms to toss out of the bucket. Along with all these pictures pasted around, she has hung Jesus on the cross, a newspaper article about a dead Kumiai woman found outside a bar in Oakland, and puffy-faced angels cut from magazines. Then there are programs announcing the order of service that she got from the church, and powwow leaflets, and pasted-together signs she made from paper plates and a thick black marker. At night, she reads them to me: *Keep Out, deliberate, DE Liberate, Berate, Delicately berate!!! They are coming!! Be warned!! Chief Joseph will save us! Make Bread Now!* Around all this are cutouts of devils and gargoyles, chimeras and totem poles. The makeshift wallpaper runs completely around the living room walls.

Mami gives up cleaning. We don't cook anymore, either, just open the cans of soup or spaghetti and eat them with our fingers. They lie around half-finished, among the clothes and furniture and records. Now, when the phone rings, Mami pulls the plug from the wall and buries the phone under piles of clothes. "I won't let them get to us," she says. "Don't you worry, angel."

FOURTEEN

I wake to a rattle, the door pumping inward at the frame, a knock so loud it frightens me, my heart beats furiously. They have come. I step across the cans of soup lined up around the sofa, the piles of clothes barricading the door, and peek through the hole in the plastic covering the window. I expect a monster, a pair of small twins arriving to steal our souls. But it is Arlie, in her nurse's scrubs. All over her blouse, little cartoon dogs dressed as doctors listen to each other's hearts with miniature stethoscopes.

"Lee. Amalie, you open up this door, you hear? Open it up!"

I look back at Mami; she's asleep near the television. Her hair is stiffened where she soaked it in alcohol to wash out the demons.

"Amalie!"

But Mami doesn't stir. I lean my chin on the windowsill, widen the plastic circle with my fingers until the hole is large enough to reach my arm through. The air is icy cold outside. The wet fuzz on my arm stands up like tiny icicles. My whole body sweats, my hair sticks to the back of my neck. The heat is turned up so high that I feel dizzy. I think about opening the door. She doesn't look like a monster. Grampa seemed to trust her, and she made all the spots on me go away. I reach through the plastic toward her, almost touching, but she doesn't see me.

"Damn it," she whispers, sucks in a deep breath and leans her forehead against the door. I feel sorry for her then. She looks so sad, and why can't I open the door for her?

My head is woozy and all my thoughts slide into one another, so that all inside me feels slippery. She turns to leave and as she gets halfway down the steps, she blurs, as if walking away in a dream, and I call out her name quietly.

"Hi, Arlie."

She turns around, walks swiftly up to the window, and rips the plastic in a frenzy.

"Jesus Christ, Alice, you're in there? Holy Mother of God, look at you, child."

She reaches through the plastic and slides her hands under my arms, pulling me through the window. The icy air collides sharply with my slick skin, and I feel as if I've been smacked. Everything swirls, a pain whirls around my head.

"Look at me, baby," she's saying, tilting my chin up, "look at me."

But I feel as if my insides have turned green, as if I'm fading and maybe this is how it feels, my soul being pulled from me. She leans me against the steps and peers through the window.

"Oh God, oh God almighty, come on, child."

And then we are at the gas station and Arlie is calling the police.

"No," I cry. "No, don't call them! Please, they'll take her away, please!"

"Hush, child," she says, "they won't, they won't."

Arlie doesn't tell them about me when they unlock the door for her. She makes Mami take pills in a paper cup, and she goes through the house with a trash bag, throwing things in, swearing, and making the cross in front of her face. "Oh, child," she says, whenever she looks at me. "Good God."

She opens all the doors so the stench is suddenly present to me, now that the fresh air is coming in. When she's cleared a path, she helps Mami to the kitchen table, presses a cool washcloth to her face, and arranges the chairs so that the two of them face each other. She looks into Mami's eyes, and speaks kindly.

"Lee, I'm going to tell you this now, honey. I'm going to call social services tomorrow. I'm going to call, you hear me?"

Mami nods, even smiles at her. She's still smiling when she closes the door gently behind Arlie, and packs a bag, holds it open for me. I put inside it: my doll, my charms, my earring. Together we lock up the door, and start walking.

FIFTEEN

We spend the night in a park. I'm warm under Mami's shawls and a blanket, my head resting on a plastic bag full of clothes that is soft but sticks to my cheek. In the middle of the night I wake up sweaty, the moisture from my cheek running in little lines down the bag's creases. The streetlights in the distance make the grass look blue and fuzzy. Mami is sitting up, her arm, curled around my shoulder, falls limply when I turn to look up at her. I watch her eyes moving rapidly behind the lids, her cheek sometimes twitching. I lift her arm, pull it back around me and slip back to sleep.

When I wake, the air is warm and the day bright. We've slept past morning. Far off, the sounds of a breaking piñata and children laughing. A nearby trash can attracts colorful flies, specks of green and black that pinch my cheek and buzz around my ears, tickling when they land. I swat at one and watch it zigzag away. I'm thirsty, so Mami finds a water fountain near the public restrooms, a solid block of concrete with a foot pedal that she lifts me up against. I drink in breathless gulps, wetting my nose and eyelashes in the unwieldy stream of water.

Near the picnic tables, where the piñata swung, I pick up a piece of candy in a bright wrapper.

When I try to put it in my mouth, Mami smacks the melting red licorice from my hand. "Don't swallow it, don't swallow."

I try to pick it up again.

"Poison," Mami hisses.

I start to cry.

"No, don't cry," she says. "I won't let anything happen to you, angel. Don't cry."

"Why are they trying to get me?" I ask her.

"Maybe they're not, baby. I just can't figure it out."

"They're probably not," I say. "Okay?"

We take off our shoes and walk around the lake. There are tiny bugs and wildflowers under our bare feet. I stop crying and Mami plays with me in the park. We slide and roll down the hill. The sprinklers are going, the grass just cut, the bristly leaves of the bushes still stiff from landscaping. By noon, the sun has settled overhead, painting the grass a painful glare-green.

We race to the swings. On Mami's lap, I swing over a steep hill. She wraps her arms around my waist as we swing high, leaning back together to face the sun. It feels like home. We swing forward, her legs kicking beneath me, chains creaking, our hair flying, and rise up high again. Then Mami's arms open, as if it has suddenly occurred to them to set me free. At the highest point, in a mask of sunlight, her knees shift slightly under me.

She lets me go.

I hit the gravel. The world comes in quieter, the dampened sound of children laughing far away, the rush of leaves in the trees. I want my mother. I pick myself up slowly and bits of gravel fall from my knees, leaving small round specks of blood. I panic. I can't find her. Across the park, I see a baseball field, black hair in the bleachers, a flannel shirt. I have found her. I run and run. But up close I can see that this is not my mother at all. It's a strange woman staring back at me, motioning to people nearby. I panic, run back toward the swings, for the concrete shelter of the public restrooms nearby.

Mami is inside, crouched over the toilet in an open stall. I sob, and she looks up at me, but without recognition. She is crying, too. I go and stand next to her. We cry together, cry hard and very much like each other. I hit her, dent her chest and shoulders with tight fists. She grabs me. Her wild hands push my arms into the basin. The water turns pink. Her eyes are strange, as if looking at something far off. But I see nothing in the water, just the gash on my arm blooming red.

There they all are. The faces of people, alight with shock and pity. People from the baseball field gathered around the door to look at us. The woman kneeling at the toilet, beside her a dirty child, knees and arms wet and bleeding.

I curl my feet under me, hold my mother hard. Maybe we see differently, but our two faces must match, eyes swelling, caught like moths flying into headlights.

In the emergency room, we sit in a row of metal chairs. The policemen are hovering by a nurses' station, pointing at Mami sometimes, and talking into the radios pulled from their belts. My eyes are drying and I feel as if I'm waking up, as if my head is clearing. I wipe my face and nose with my shirt. Tiny specks of dried blood flake off, and I notice the red pattern on my T-shirt. It is the shape of a curling leaf or a flame. I unfold Mami's arm, wipe a place clean with an imaginary swab, and tell her it won't hurt. Then I make a needle of my thumb and forefinger, poke her forearm and fold her arm up to stop the blood. "There, now," I say. "Aren't you brave?"

Finally, a plump woman behind a glass pane motions for us to come back while she gets a policeman. "Come through here," she points to a heavy wooden door beside her, then gets off her stool and holds it open for us. She eyes my damp T-shirt, my surfacing bruises. "Let's sit you down here for a minute." She lifts me onto a table and I hold Mami's hand as she goes behind the doors and comes back with a policeman and a pretty doctor.

The doctor reaches for my cheek. "How are you holding up, sweetie?" She bends to face me, but I turn to Mami. Mami looks at me carefully, and then slowly turns to the doctor. Her mouth hangs open. Her eyes are wide and clear.

"Is she going to be okay?"

"Yes," the doctor says, looking at Mami distractedly, "yes, she is going to be fine."

The policeman flips the first few pages on his clipboard. He writes while the doctor is talking. Then he turns the clipboard over to show me a sad face he has drawn. The doctor dabs cotton on my knee and it stings.

"Is this your daughter?" the policeman asks.

Mami fingers the bruises on my arm. She looks at me. "No," she says. "No, she's no relation at all."

SIXTEEN

I press the undershirt tight against my chest, curled away from this woman, and work the fabric under my fingertips. Somewhere on this shirt there is a thread that will pull everything taut. There is a beginning knot nailed into the dirt with a weaving stick or looped through the needle of our old sewing machine, and the string trails limply behind me, telling the story of how I got here.

The woman leans in with her palm open, asking for my shirt. Her powdery perfume warms the air around me. "Don't you want me to take that for you?" she says. "Get it nice and clean?"

I shake my head firmly no. It is a fine network of breakable threads. If the wrong one is pulled I will be lost, spinning and spinning out of the story.

But where? Which one? Which thread? One of the ragged pieces pilled with dried blood? Around the collar hem where the cotton daisies are peeling away, falling into my lap?

135

She must have come here for me in the middle of the night: I woke up in her arms. The air smelled of the inky coffee that she held in her hand and the carbon papers that littered a desk nearby. I climbed off her lap and squeezed into a corner, my cheek against the cool metal of a green filing cabinet. And she waited for me, keys jangling against her hip, hesitant eyes, and there was only this undershirt to hold on to.

I am tired. But if I sleep again, in whose arms will I wake up? The undershirt is bloodstained and graying. I make a tight ball of it in my fist. The cool cabinet sends a chill down my bare chest. I won't let her have it. I am afraid of going back, of all these threads knotted into the shirt yanking me back to that park, to the faces of all of those people staring at us, to the inside of the ambulance with its alcohol smell and red, red colors everywhere, to the man who walked us into the hospital. Still, I want to stay tethered.

I can't go back there, but I want to hold on. Maybe *this* is a dream, and I will close my eyes and go on dreaming. When I wake again, I will have dreamed it all: the hospital, my dented knees, this woman, this carbon- and coffee-smelling office.

The woman snakes a freckled white arm behind the filing cabinet and tugs on my shoulder. I look into her face. It's a soft face. Like Arlie, she's just a fuzzy figure in a dream. "I'm sleepy," I tell her, holding on to her pale neck when she lifts me.

"Of course," she says. "It's been a long day for you, honey. But it's okay now, you'll see."

Outside in a parking lot, she opens the door of a station wagon and settles me into the back. On the sticky vinyl seat next to me is already a small girl, just a little taller than me. When she turns to me, I can see white-blond hairs plastered in moist ringlets to her reddened cheeks. She's been crying.

"See, silly girls," the woman says, "there's nothing to be afraid of."

What happens when I get big like her and the undershirt doesn't fit me anymore? Will I still be able to go back? I curl into the T-shirt, breathe its familiar smell, and rest my cheek on the nubby cotton.

Eyes closed, I tell myself the story. *When I was a little girl, I met a condor . . . When I was a little girl, a condor stole me away. No . . . it starts . . . I met a condor and he said to me*—but I can't remember.

The fuzzy-haired woman looks at us in the rearview mirror. She says, "Anne, honey, help Alice buckle the seat belt."

The little girl leans over and fastens me in. She stares at my balled-up undershirt. Is that her father with the lit-blue eyes and rough gray hair? He wears a thick white shirt and a loosened tie. They don't look like anyone I know, not Grampa, not Mami, not even Arlie. "She didn't have anything with her?" he says. The woman shakes her head. She wrinkles her face and winces. "Not even a *sweater.*"

I lean my forehead against the door; there is leftover rain on the window, a quiet darkness and a moist heat inside the car. I feel the little girl staring at me. When I stare back, she smiles, reaches across the seat and links her pinkie in mine. Her fingers are blotchy and pale.

It's okay for now; holding on to this shirt. I let myself sleep.

When I wake again I'm under a lacy white blanket, its scalloped edges scratching my cheek. The sheets underneath are pulled taut around my feet. I keep my eyes closed, listening to the sound of steady breathing beside me. For a moment I am home and Mami is beside me. But the breathing is too soft-sounding and quick to be Mami's. When I open my eyes I see that it is just the little girl, her head turned into my shoulder, her legs hanging limply off the edge of the bed. I trip getting out of bed and see that I'm wearing a nightgown, its fuzzy hem too long for me. It's a pink room, with soft white carpet, a little white vanity table with a matching mirror and stool. Flowered wallpaper, a stack of clothes folded neatly on top of a dresser. And in the hallway: bright, bright walls and a strange yellow-striped wallpaper. A long corridor ending in stairs. There are pictures on the wall; all people I do not know. A shining wooden floor that's slippery. A clock that's taller than me.

I sit down on the floor. I'm sorry now. I'm sorry and I want to go back, back to the hospital, back to the park, back to Mami. I close my eyes again, try to go back. *When I was a little girl,* I whisper, *a condor stole me away.*

And then there is the woman in a white robe at the end of the hallway, smiling and calling me darling. "Good morning," she's saying, setting a stack of towels on a shelf in a hallway closet. "Sleep okay, darling?"

She would know. Where is Mami? But I can't ask her; I don't want to *be* in this story.

"What is it?" She's coming closer. "Don't cry, darling." She takes my hand and walks me into a bathroom. The walls are so bright. She flicks a light on and it hurts my eyes. Where is my undershirt?

She presses a cold washcloth to my cheeks and forehead. "Anne loves to have a bath," she says. "She just likes the water. How about you?" She turns on the faucet. "You're going to feel so much better once you're all nice and clean." She lifts the nightgown over my head. "We'll have to get you some new nightgowns, won't we? Anne's are just a little too big." She puts her cold hands under my arms and lifts me into the tub. "I'm sure she wouldn't mind if you played with her toys." She sets a little boat in the water and sails it toward me.

"What? What is it, honey?"

I don't *belong* in this story. The water is too hot. It burns. But I can't speak to her. I am going back, back to Mami. I haven't forgotten her. I haven't let go.

The woman guides my head back under the faucet, her hand cradling my neck. I close my eyes as the water rushes over me. I am Kwikumat in water. I am at the beginning of the story, on my way to Mami. But when I open my eyes, the woman is still there, and shampoo suds leak into my eyelashes. "Are you warm enough?" she says. She puts a warm washcloth on my back and rubs.

Condor, tricking me, wrong story.

"Don't you want to talk to me, honey?"

She wraps a towel around me and lifts me out. "You don't understand what's going on," she says. "Do you?" She shifts me onto her hip. "Poor darling." She is so warm and soft. I let my head fall into her chest. Little dust clouds of baby powder hang in the air between us. She sets me down and rubs the towel over my head. I step into a pair of underwear, too big for me. "Well, at least we know this will fit," she says. When I lift my arms into the air, she pulls an under-shirt over me and my stomach goes light and fluttery. It's *my* under-shirt. Only, it's bright white now, the color of the walls. There are no orange soda stains, no bits of crusty black blood, no trace of any part of us. I scream when the woman touches me. The man with the blue eyes appears in the doorway. He has both of his arms around me when I bite him. I bite down hard, feeling the release of some softness on my teeth. He jerks his arm and lets me go. I run down the stairs, looking for a way out. I run into a kitchen, throw down all the things I can reach—plates, knives, a cookie jar. The sound of shrieking brakes, of bells ringing, the dull thud of the cookie jar cracking in two.

Here is a door. A way out. It's some kind of yard. On the other side of a screen, there are rows of rubber boots lined up neatly, a pool and a garden. I pull the shirt over my head. I want to bury it. I kneel in the garden among flower bushes. Paper-thin blossoms whirl in the air around me as I dig. But the dirt *won't* come up. I rake and scrape with my fingers. My nails fill with dirt. I snap up pieces of grass and spread them over the shirt, push through the fabric into the dirt underneath. But it won't go. It's sprawled flat on top of the grass.

The man and woman are together by the door, watching me. And the little girl is standing near me in a pale blue nightgown and bare feet. "I'll help you," she says softly. She turns to face the door and says, "Can we bury it, Mom?"

With a plastic beach shovel we slice into the dry dirt and pull up enough to cover the shirt. I tamp the dirt down over the shirt with my palms. The little girl sits with her legs crossed next to me.

And after a while, we go inside. We sit at a table, the little girl and I. In front of us are plates of scrambled eggs and identical small glasses of orange juice. But I won't eat. I'm going back, back inside the story, back through the threads of my shirt.

The eggs sit inside little settled clouds of steam. I lean close to them, and the warmth moistens my cheek. *Are you hungry, little girl? I'll feed you, little girl.*

The taste is warm and sweet in my mouth before I realize what I've done. My face is wet and cold. I push my fingers into the tight flesh of my stomach until I feel the little half moons of my fingernails and vomit.

Down so deep, I'm in a barrel. Wood presses against my shoulders, and above: a condor is scratching, scratching.

But when I lift my forehead from the sticky red-and-white tablecloth, there is the woman who made the sound with her keys, the man with the lit-up eyes, and the little girl.

SEVENTEEN

I watch Mrs. Warrick as she moves around the kitchen, dragging a torn rag soaked in ammonia across the countertops. Her pale, staticky hair stands up all around her face. Unlike Mami, who cleaned in a hurry with the radio turned as loud as it would go, Mrs. Warrick is slow and careful. She seems relaxed, working her way calmly around the kitchen. She cranes her head back to me from where she stands near the window, wringing the rag into the sink. "Do you want to help, Alice?"

I climb the kitchen chair she pulls out for me, and plug the drain. I like to watch the water fill slowly, the bubbles rising until a soapy prism obscures the bottom of the sink.

"You know, you're the only kid I know who likes to clean so much." She turns the water off and lowers the dishes into the sink for me. The house is quiet. Mr. Warrick and Anne have gone to the dentist, and then to Anne's dance class. A light rain has grayed the

143

sky outside. Through the window above the sink, I watch an old green house across the street. The windows are always dark there. There is never a light on in any room, not even at night. A delicate, small-boned old woman in a housedress stands at the top of the porch steps with a shopping cart steadied on her hip. She tugs and tugs, until it rolls back and throws her off-balance. Mrs. Warrick leans in next to me, her wispy hair tickling my cheek, her rubber gloves dripping. "Poor old Mrs. Snow," she sighs. "She had kids, I hear, but they wouldn't come to see her, and now they're all gone."

I lean my chin on Mrs. Warrick's shoulder, make a widening ring of circles in the dishwater.

"Does she live there all alone?"

"Yes, I think so. Not a soul to take care of her."

I wonder if a person could settle in like that; know that she will always have with her the bones she grew up with, the fingers that cuddled her knees. Could I? I make a soapy tornado in the water.

"How long have I been here?" I ask.

Mrs. Warrick peels her yellow rubber glove from her hand and drops it in the sink. Then she walks to the calendar on the refrigerator and flips a page. "Four weeks and one day."

It feels longer. It is the time it takes to forget the pattern of wrinkles on Grampa's face, to taste boiled beans, to chase the image of a face that's fading like water evaporating on cement. This house, this neighborhood, even the inside of their car is quiet. Outside there is no noise, not even at night. The furniture is covered in thick plastic.

The walls are plain, painted bright white with nothing hanging on them. There are eight rooms and another one outside for the car. There is a pool in the ground and a garden of sharp-beaked flowers and squat and lazy palm fronds. Everywhere in the house smells like lemon. I sleep in Anne's room, and since yesterday, I have my own bed. Mr. Warrick dresses in suits, blue or black ones with thick, striped ties. He leaves for work in the morning while we're all still in our nightgowns. "Good-bye, girls," he says, and always makes the same joke. "When I'm gone you can all go back to bed." But we don't go to bed, we eat breakfast and do chores. Sweep the floor, collect the laundry, take all the tiny knickknacks, miniature vases, and figurines off the shelves and dust them with old pillowcases. When it's dark, Mr. Warrick comes home and looks through a telescope he built himself. Twice, we get to sit with him, and look through it at the stars. I don't think much of Mami. I think of digging, and of what there is to be scared of that I cannot see. But it is as if everything is asleep, here. Sometimes I think I'm asleep, too, dreaming all of this. But each morning, I wake up still here.

I stack the plates on the other side of the sink and Mrs. Warrick lifts me off the chair. I go into the living room and stand on the long sofa. It's lodged against the window. Standing on the couch and reaching up on my tiptoes, I can see the green house. Just beside the house are two small headstones, sagging and chipped. The sun has gone down and the streetlights are making fuzzy triangles on the sodden porch. But there are still no lights inside.

145

"She's blind, Alice, she doesn't need the lights," Mr. Warrick finally says when he walks through the front door with Anne. They drip water onto the plastic carpet runner, and Mrs. Warrick makes them take off their wet coats and shoes. Anne runs upstairs in her pink tights and leotard and Mr. Warrick drops his keys in a bowl on a side table near the door. He lifts me off the sofa. "Have you been watching all night?" I don't want to answer, don't want to speak at all. The old woman's house makes me shiver inside. I squeeze my eyes closed tight.

"What did you do today, Little Alice? Why don't you tell us what's always going on in that head? Did you help Mrs. Warrick?"

"Yes," Mrs. Warrick says softly. She wipes her hands on a towel. "She's a good little helper." She leans in to kiss Mr. Warrick on the cheek. "Wash up," she says to me. "Dinner soon."

I go upstairs and close the bathroom door, but I cannot stop thinking about the green house. If you are blind, and the lights in your house are always out, how do you understand what things are? Underneath the sink, under a broken tile, I feel for the matchbook I've hidden. I scrape the last match until it lights, then sit on the toilet to watch it burn.

I remember a time in Papi's trailer on the reservation. It was quiet when I woke and there was no noise except the faucet dripping. I went through each room looking for Mami and Papi. They had gone to the liquor store sometime in the morning while I was asleep. The floor trembled when a truck passed on the road. In my nightgown, I went out in the dark morning and walked barefoot to the community center. Tia Jimenez found me there, trying to call Mami on the pay phone.

She walked me home and she sang to me while we waited for Mami. It was a night chant, a long cycle like the lightning song. A story about an old woman who comes to meet you just before you are born. When you try to look back toward mystery, she blows smoke in your face so that you cannot see. The old woman shades the place you've come from so that you won't be confused between waking and dreaming. Tia Jimenez had taken a deep drag from her cigarette, and blown a gust of smoke in my face. I giggled, watching her wrinkled fingers through the smoke. "How many?" she said, holding up two fingers, then three. "How many now?"

But what is it *Mrs. Snow* cannot see? What is it you're shielded from when you leave home? Waking or Dreaming?

EIGHTEEN

We're under the covers with a flashlight, the strands of Anne's wispy hair floating up around her temples, glowing in the warm yellow light. Mr. Warrick has brought us books on cartography from the university library, old road maps from garage sales, and diagrams of archaeological digs. There are photos of buried treasure, whole cities petrified, people and animals dug out of the ground and photographed. As I run my hands across the pictures, the lumps of mud imprinted in human and animal form, I discover what I want more than anything in the world: to dig, to pull a hidden relic out of the ground and call it by name. There are steps leading up to the tops of stone temples, timelines and animal tracks, the remnants of entire cities. The small blocks of mud imprinted with human fingerprints and animal form look as if the near dead stopped on their way to God to press their faces into the dirt.

All summer, Anne and I dig together, making maps from each

intersection of the neighborhood back to the house and pinning them up around our room. We've counted the steps from the house to the graveyard behind Mrs. Snow's house, from the car to the door, from the bedroom to the basement. We've been digging mostly in the yard around the house, looking for secrets. Underneath the dry top layers where the dirt is moist, we've found the discarded shells of molting insects, stubborn knotted roots anchoring the slightest of stems and the beginnings of sunflowers. The best harvest is near the sump pump, where there are chips of green glass from broken bottles, the plastic ring of a pacifier, and once, a school picture of Anne with her hands folded on top of a fake tree limb and her hair in neat pigtails.

I run my fingers across the pictures of bone fragments, and something that feels like hunger twists inside me. I go to the window and draw the curtain. Mrs. Snow's little headstones are sagging into the dirt. "We should dig near those headstones," I tell Anne.

"What if we dig up bones?" she says.

"So," I say. "Bones are *people.*"

"Bones are dead people, screwball." She flicks the covers off her head. "Aren't you scared of dead people?"

"Uh-uh." I want to find bones, to find evidence of people rooted in the earth. I am sure that these bones could *grow.*

Anne says, "Giirrr." She flicks the flashlight on under her chin and crosses her eyes.

"Kwikumat made life from the bones in the dirt," I say. "What would happen if we watered them and let them grow?"

Anne falls backward on the bed, making googly eyes. "Giirrr," she says, "I'm dead."

"Come on." I tug on her feet. "Let's go."

"No way," Anne says. But she is smiling, pulling her pink bunny slippers onto her feet. She holds her arms out like a zombie and follows me down the hall. We put our hooded jackets on over our pajamas. I remember Mami telling me stories of how Mamita's uncles used skulls. They could talk through them to the ancestors. Through the way the wind rattled them, through a fly that might land on them, through the shape of the bitten leaves put inside them, the skulls whispered secrets. I want a skull, a whole collection of skulls. I want to take them home and decorate our room with them, but Anne takes my face in her hands and makes me swear that if we find any, I won't try to take them home. Already, the walls in our room are covered with maps, the ones I copied from the atlas Mr. Warrick brought home and the timelines we drew of our "phases": the stuffed animal phase, the cereal period. We have a Mexican map with tiny bare footprints in every direction and an old sea map with mermaids and giant fish in its boiling ocean.

We tiptoe down the hall and crack her parents' bedroom door, making sure they're asleep. We get the flashlight and our beach shovels. Anne links her arm in mine when we get outside. All the lights in the housing development are out and the night is cool and quiet. A dog barks at us and we freeze until he stops. Halfway across the street, we start giggling. "You first," Anne says, pushing me ahead.

151

"Shh!" I say. "Did you hear that?"

"What?"

"Just kidding!"

"What if they wore eyeglasses?" Anne says. "Will they still have their glasses on?"

"I don't think so." I unravel the picture of Aztec bones I've cut from the newspaper and shine the flashlight on it. It's worn at the creases, coming apart from being too long in the pocket of my shorts or the inside of my shoe. In the photograph, a skeleton stares out from the bottom of a sunken tower, his face tilted up as if he were posing for the camera. A circle of stones is stacked around him neatly. He lies there in the dirt, *just so,* folded up awkwardly, hugging himself into the space.

Anne shines the flashlight on the picture. "I wonder how they found him," she says.

I imagine Abel picking up a strange-looking rock. One that was painted maybe, or unusually smooth. Maybe he'd picked it up before, and put it back without ever knowing that underneath him were the bones of an entire family. A whole life buried underneath and forgotten, and all that's left: just bones like the skeleton staring up at us from the ruins in the picture as if to say, *You, up there, look, I'm here, waiting, waiting for you.*

"That's what I want to do," I say.

She looks at me with raised eyebrows. "Get buried in a pyramid?"

"No. I want to be an archaeologist helping old bones."

"But do they put them back?" she says.

"What?"

"The bones. The ones the archaeologists dig up."

"Of course!" I say, but I'm not so sure. I remember the bird bones Papi dug out of the ground on the reservation, how I could see the faint lines etched into the dull ivory-yellow surfaces. They looked like road maps winding around the skull. Did they put those back?

I dig first by the sagging headstone, tracing my finger along the dates carved into the stone. How can the bones grow in there, trapped under the stone like strangled roots? Someone has left wildflowers around it that are withered and dry, and weeds are clinging to it. The dirt comes up easily, but all I find is a dusty novena card with a name scrawled on it. I put it into my jacket pocket and pull my hood over my head.

"What do you think dead people look like?" says Anne. "Do they have hair?"

"After you die," I tell her. "Your hair keeps growing."

"How do you know?"

"Your dad told me."

When Anne isn't looking, I put my face down near the dirt to smell it. There is something so familiar about it, the smell of dirt from someplace with Mami. But places are becoming blurry in my memory. I dig a hole for my picture of bones. "Poor boy," I whisper, dropping handfuls of dirt onto the photograph until it's covered. "You're just dry bones."

The dog starts barking again. Anne tugs on my sleeve. "Let's go," she says. "I've got the creeps."

I follow her back to the house, watching the flashlight make shapes along the street. We go to the backyard and lay on our backs to watch the stars. Once, in the rain, we came out here with Mr. Warrick to watch a meteor shower. We drank hot chocolate together, huddled under a big umbrella. "You know, girls, the stars are maps too," Mr. Warrick told us. "Even the earliest mapmakers understood the importance of stargazing. They're like lighthouses," he said. "People have been making maps from them for thousands of years. And not just paper maps. So many yarns knotted, so many sticks woven together, and there you have it: the wave patterns surrounding the Polynesian islands, the Inca trading route, the compass for a ship in the night." But tonight the stars look like freckles, scattered about in no particular pattern. The grass is cool on my back, and the night is quiet. I match my breath to Anne's, count the stars, and try to see the maps.

NINETEEN

On the morning of Anne's twelfth birthday, the windows are covered in ash. When we lift the bedroom window, soft gray flecks whirl in the warm morning air like falling snow. The air outside is thick and dry. It smells like burning wood. When I stick my tongue out, it tastes like fire. Anne leans out the window. "Look at the cars!" I spot the Warricks' station wagon in the carport downstairs. It's completely covered; an opaque blanket of fuzzy ash covers the windshield, the trunk, even the tires. I draw a line in the ash across the windowsill and smudge it on Anne's cheek. She giggles. We're in our underwear. We slept on top of the blankets last night, with fans blowing and wet rags on our foreheads and chests. It is so hot that Anne and I have spent all summer in only our bathing suits, putting them on first thing in the morning and wearing them all day. The fires started in July. Hot Santa Ana winds blew in and kindled small blazes everywhere. By August, they had spread through the counties around us. One fire burned for three days, through two neighbor-hoods, harvesting a whole development of houses. It climbed uphill, eating up fuel, and consumed a development of new townhomes in the valley, each with its own twelve-foot wooden porch. I've been watching on television, flicking through the channels searching for the pictures of ordinary things lit up and changing, for the little porches collapsing. I've been sneaking down the stairs late at night, turning the volume down, looking in the images for that exact moment when things break apart and spill out their magic. Now the smoke is in the air, warm and comforting.

We get dressed quickly and go out to the driveway. We walk across the burning asphalt, holding hands; making wet footprints and watching them dry up in the sun. We write our names on all the car windows. On the front windshield of the station wagon, I write, *Happy Birthday Anne!* Sometimes, lately, I forget I haven't always been here and that Anne is not really my family. I close my eyes and think, Tomorrow I'll leave. I'll go back.

"Aunt Lilly is afraid you'll be a bad influence on her girls," Anne whispers. "I heard Mom talking about it on the phone." Aunt Lilly's girls come in a van with their parents. One is Laurie and the other Amanda. They carry pink suitcases with twirling ballerinas stenciled onto the front. They're twelve and thirteen with slight breasts and long red hair, rippling from loosened braids. Their faces are frenzies of white and red, and their skin is freckled all over. We follow them upstairs where they stop in front of our bedroom door. "Oh God,"

Laurie says. "It's like, a *child's* room." She drops her suitcase on the floor and runs her fingers across the topographical map on the dresser. "What's all this?" she says. I shut the maps I've drawn into Anne's desk drawer. After cake and the birthday song, we take our towels to the backyard and leave them in a pile on the patio table. I wade in with my arms crossed around me, hiding my flat chest. Anne and her cousins stay on the lawn chairs, giggling and working lotion onto their shoulders. I float on my back in the shallow end. Bits of ash are floating in the pool. Trapping them in my palm, I rub my fingers together and watch the debris liquefy into dirty water. Anne sweeps around the pool. "You're twelve now," Amanda says, "do you have your period yet?" Laurie laughs.

"Come and get some Cokes," Mrs. Warrick calls from the sliding doors, and Anne follows her inside.

"So, do you have a boyfriend?" Amanda says.

"You don't *have* to talk to Alice," Laurie says. "She's not even family." Amanda giggles.

"Her mother's crazy," Laurie says. "No really, like *loony* birds. Anne told me, that's why they had to let her live with them."

I turn to face them, shame burning me. Why would Anne tell them this?

Laurie says, "Is your mother really crazy?"

I don't answer, just buckle my knees, and let the water pool over my head. I swim out as far as I can, kick until I feel the bottom of the pool, then I turn and let the water lap against my cheeks; keep my ears plugged so that I hear nothing. I seal my eyelids shut and fold my arms across my ribs.

In the beginning there was only water. This earth did not exist, only the watery depths, this place I can see when my eyes are closed. The first place, before Kwikumat came with sickness and death, and pulled us each from the murky waters. I stay hidden under the surface, wishing for a way back to things I never knew: my grandmother gathering juncus leaves in the knee-deep water at dawn; my mother, a girl in braids, dancing at powwow. I imagine I'm living inside a dream. When I wake, I will have dreamed everything, my whole life. I will swim through to some place I remember where Mami and I are alone. A cord of fire through the water connects me to her. I feel her burn in my bones. Am I crazy, too?

At night, I dream I'm a ghost in the flames, a *mar'uk* without flesh, without bones. I can dance, agile and swift like a flame. I have the jumping magic that bounces and leaps like a spark.

Sometimes I remember the reservation in my dreams. The hazy shadow of Tia Jimenez drifts above me, the lines on her face carved around her brows and mouth like deep mud-slicked ravines, her tattoos faint, almost faded away. She doesn't speak, but tugs on my arms, pats me on the back as if to say *Get up, Get up.* I feel dizzy, my head pounding and my chest tight and compressed. But I rise and take her arm. She walks wobbly and unsure. On the other side of the hill, where I first saw the bones of birds, she points to a fire. It has jumped a small creek and the sparks are whirling in the wind like red snow.

Kwe'xuyaw nyaKwe'xu'yaw, she says. Sweat forms in my hairline. The smell of smoke is all around. The fire is turning the dawn a faint, luminous gray. *Bonito,* Tia Jimenez says. *It's beautiful.* The clouds are curling like the edges of smoking paper, and already the silvery black of burned earth is visible around us. Tia Jimenez sings the lightning song. But I don't understand her Quechan. I close my hand in hers and hold on.

Other times I have nightmares. I hear voices calling me, something closing in all around me until I wake up sweaty and panicked. There is something here in the water, underneath the world, that feels like home.

I push off the bottom, suck in air at the surface, and then sink back down. Crazy I say the word underwater. It's the first time I've heard it pronounced, this label. But crazy does not contain her. It changes her into something different.

When I reach the surface again, Anne swims out, grabs my feet and sinks them so that I have to stop floating on my back.

"What's wrong?" She looks annoyed. "Come in and play with us."

I narrow my eyes, though I do not blame her. "Go without me," I say. Floating on my back again, I wonder about Mami, about Anne and Mrs. Snow and Tia Jimenez. How much are we the same? How much different?

TWENTY

Mrs. Warrick drives us in the station wagon to school, a big building, surrounded by two playgrounds and a soccer field. Anne and I stand together at the door to the classroom while Mrs. Warrick talks to the teacher. She wears a dress with a bib front and suspenders.

"Is this one yours?" she asks, pointing to Anne. Anne and her mother look alike. Their white-blond hair is wispy, almost translucent and their skin is pale with blue veins showing through around their eyes. Mrs. Warrick pulls me into her, and I wrap my arms around her waist.

"Actually, they're both mine." She hugs me, then holds me by the shoulders at arm's length and says, "You girls go ahead in." We step inside the classroom, but with the door open, I can hear them talking. "Alice is a foster child," Mrs. Warrick is saying. "She's quiet, a little shy. She comes from an Indian family." There are name tags on the desks, and Anne and I end up three rows away from each other.

161

There is a library corner and an aquarium, and in the far corner where I fix my eyes, a relief map with blue and brown mountains rising out of the grids and shapes.

Once we're all seated, the teacher tells us her name is Miss Morgan, and then asks us all to introduce ourselves. Anne is called on before me. She says she dances ballet; she's in the Girl Scouts. Anne knows most of the kids already, but when Miss Morgan asks her to demonstrate first position, she shakes her head shyly.

Before I stand, Miss Morgan smiles. "Alice, what can you tell us about Indians?"

I stand, lean against my desk. My ears burn.

When I don't say anything, she folds her hands on her stomach, comes closer to me. "For instance, what are some of your traditional foods?"

At the Warricks', we eat pancakes and frozen dinners, sometimes baked ham and cake after church with bright green peas and neon-colored Kool-Aid.

It's so quiet. I concentrate on the shuffle of feet behind me, on a pen tapping a desk nearby. But she doesn't let me sit down. I stare at the pile of books on my desk: reading, social studies, math.

"Sweetie?" Miss Morgan says.

A memory of Tia Jimenez; pots boiling on the stove, damp mesquite flour. "Mesquite beans," I suggest.

I hear a boy's laugh behind me. Miss Morgan says, "Thank you, Alice. Andrew, let's hear something about you."

Out on the playground at recess, the boys collect dry leaves and sagebrush. They dump the leaves over my head, smashing them into my hair.

"Ding, ding, ding, time for dinner," the laughing one says. "Want some leaves? How about some grass?"

Anne has found her friends from last year, other blond girls with pigtails. They wear bright plastic headbands and flared-leg jeans. As I'm picking leaves from my hair, Anne sets down the jump rope she's turning and runs over, followed by the other girls. She calls, "Leave my sister alone."

I stare quietly at my feet.

"Your sister!" One of the boys laughs. "She doesn't look like your sister!"

Anne suddenly screams. "A bee!" she says, swatting frantically.

I flick it from her elbow.

"They're just ignorant," Anne says, offering me a handle of the jump rope. I shrug, try to smile at them. But I want to go back to searching. I'm looking for the right place, a place hidden from the playground and from the doors where the teachers and lunchroom monitors jangle their key rings, drink their coffees and talk with one another.

I have three matchsticks hidden in the bottom of my backpack, and I want to light them, drag the tips across the cement playground and hold the flame to my knucklebone or heat a pinecone. I know from Mami that pinecones need the heat. They can't survive without it. The pinecone will glow inside a fire and explode, sending pieces of life out all over to grow. Without the heat, the pinecone stays quiet, keeps all its life locked up inside. I give the rope to another girl, and walk across the playground. I tear sheets of paper from my spiral notebook and light them with a match drawn on the concrete. I hold them in my hand until the blackened paper reaches my fingers, then drop it on the cement and watch it rock. I close my eyes, inhale the familiar sulfurous smell of burning paper. I finger my burned skin, bright pink at first, then deep purple-black. An old burn on my knuckle has already turned to a wrinkled white scar on brown skin.

Something feels reachable inside me when I feel the heat on my skin. There is something missing in the texture of everyday life, and I feel it for a second, holding the paper. There are things that grow in the shape-shifting power of fire's heat. What will happen if the world stays cold? What will happen to me?

I open my eyes to the sound of someone shrieking. "What are you doing?" The recess monitor stands over me. She grabs me by the arm, drags me around to the front of the building. "Jesus, Mary, and Joseph, child!" As she drags me along, I can feel where her fingertips meet, squeezed around my arm. When she lets me go, at the principal's office, there are little half-moons from her fingernails on my wrist.

The principal is tall, wearing a navy blue suit. She sits in the chair next to me, leaning in with her hands on the upholstered arm. I fix my eyes on her fingers; watch the fluorescent light dancing in her deep purple nail polish. Her mouth is tight when she talks to me. "I am very concerned, Alice, very *concerned*. Do you have any idea how dangerous that is?" She sets me to writing an apology letter to the other students. "Explain how you might have hurt them," she says, "by playing with matches." She calls Mrs. Warrick and when she arrives, the principal moves back to the other side of her desk, sits in the oversized, swiveling chair, which she rocks from side to side. She does not smile at Mrs. Warrick, but looks at me sternly while she talks to her, explains what I've done. Then I'm told to wait in the chair outside the door, facing the secretary. Through the opened door, I can hear them clearly: Mrs. Warrick explaining: she's adopted, she's Indian, there are possibly fetal alcohol issues.

When the door opens, the principal's face is different, a mask of ugly pity.

It's quiet in the car on the way home. I rub the thin pink skin on my knuckle. The burn is ripening and it hurts. Mrs. Warrick stays in the car for a long time after I've gone inside.

When Mr. Warrick gets home they discuss me in the kitchen, then they call my social worker, Ms. Garcia.

At dinner, Mrs. Warrick says, "Ms. Garcia thinks it would be a good idea for you to learn something about where you come from, Alice, and we agree."

I stare into my plate: grayish ham in a shiny honey glaze.

"Don't you want to learn about your heritage, honey? We've

found you a class where you can learn bead craft, and Ms. Garcia knows a woman who can help you make a dress so you can learn to dance."

A punishment, it seems. "Anne's not taking bead craft," I mumble.

"You'll see, honey," Mrs. Warrick says, "you'll like it."

I eat the ham on my plate. It's too sweet and syrupy.

As we change into our nightgowns after dinner, Anne brushes her hair facing the window, so that her back is turned to me.

"It's not fair," she says. "You didn't even get punished."

"I don't even want to go. I'd rather take ballet classes with you."

But she throws the brush at the open closet, and pulls her patch-work quilt over her head.

I stay awake for most of the night. I walk down the hall, close the bathroom door behind me when everyone is sleeping, careful to keep the hinge from creaking. I turn the fan on, drop the last match into the sink with a wound bundle of toilet paper. Sometimes I think I can see Grampa or Mami in the smoke rings, their faces spinning away. But afterward, I feel empty and ashamed. I make my way down the hall to the Warricks' bedroom. I want to go in like Anne does, and ask to sleep with them, but I don't. I rest my head against the bedroom door and breathe.

TWENTY-ONE

It's an hour's drive on a damp Saturday morning to the American Indian Center in Huntington Park. The bead craft classes are held in a smelly conference room with marble floors and a long wooden table. We sit around the table, sewing plastic beads and fake turquoise onto strips of leather or belts and barrettes. My belt looks awful, the abstract design I was going for looks more like random crooked lines. It puts me in mind of Mami and how she could not sew beads. I remember the dangling cornrows falling off her turtle shawl. This makes me hate the class.

Mrs. Warrick arrives to pick me up early and idles outside in the brown station wagon while I gather my books. "How'd it go, kiddo?" she says when I get in the car. "Did you have fun?" Telling Mrs. Warrick the truth would upset her, so I keep quiet. She takes the ice-cream exit off the highway. Mr. Warrick doesn't even know about it. Once, Anne and I asked him to take the ice-cream exit and he looked at us as if we had conspired to vote him out of the family.

A woman and a teenage girl are seated in our regular booth, but Mrs. Warrick heads there anyway. The woman stands up when we approach the booth, but the girl slumps down farther and sucks her teeth.

Mrs. Warrick shakes the woman's hand and then turns to me. "Alice, this is Ms. Chavis."

"Heya," the woman says, then she turns to the girl. "Say hello, Marie."

Marie is mean looking. She wears a vinyl jacket with the name of a high school basketball team embroidered on the back and her long hair is pulled back tightly in a yellow headband, her eyes thickly lined in black eye shadow.

"This is my niece," the woman says. "She ain't very sociable today."

"Well, then." Mrs. Warrick puts her arm around me and squeezes my shoulder. "Let's get some ice cream." When she gets up to order at the counter, I follow her.

"Ms. Chavis is going to help you make a dress, Alice," Mrs. Warrick says, "so you can dance. And you can go with Marie to a pow-wow on Monday."

"But I don't even know her."

"She's in your class, honey."

"I have school on Monday."

"It's not good to be shy, Alice. It's good to make friends."

"Can Anne come, too?"

"I think one extra girl is handful enough." Mrs. Warrick laughs nervously, looks back at the booth. Then she looks me in the eyes. "Don't worry. If you want to come home, you can just call me, and I'll come get you, okay?"

The night before my next bead craft class, Mrs. Warrick takes me to the Chavises' apartment to spend the night with Marie.

When we wake in the morning, we find Marie's uncle Jimmy passed out on the couch downstairs. He's sprawled out on the ratty plaid cushions, his mouth open, one arm reaching out toward a turned-over beer can. "He's been missing for four days." Marie makes a mocking face. "Gone to Oakland with a bunch of friends to start a new life." We go back upstairs to wake Ms. Chavis and tell her.

"Is he dead?" Ms. Chavis asks.

"I don't know," Marie says, "I guess I'll go check."

"Hell, girl, I was just fooling. He's passed out is all, stinking up the place. See if he's got any money."

"I can't, Auntie, we've got to get out of here. We've got bead craft in twenty minutes."

"Just check his wallet before he wakes up. He owes us more than he'll ever have, the bastard."

"All right," Marie says. We go downstairs and stand in the kitchen while Marie counts to ten. I keep still, watching little spirals of dust rise around Jimmy's open mouth. When he snores, the dust speeds up, making a little whirling nebula. After ten seconds, we go back upstairs.

"Nothing," Marie says.

"Nothing? Are you sure? Did you check his pockets, too?"

"Yeah, I'm sure."

"All right then. Check what's in the fridge. He's likely going to eat us out of house and home."

"We've got to *go,* Auntie Bettie."

"Okay, but take the toilet paper with you."

"What?"

"Take it with you. Serves the bastard right."

We're working on shawls at bead craft. Marie is amazing. She can bead anything with ease. But my projects are awful. When we get back to the apartment, Marie's little sister Shirley is seated at the kitchen table with a plastic baggie on her head.

"Lice," Ms. Chavis says. She removes the bag and lifts a soggy strand of Shirley's hair. She waves it at Marie as if it were a pointer stick. "Sent home for the third time this week for lice. I had to leave work and get her again this morning."

Marie goes straight to her bedroom and I follow. But Ms. Chavis keeps talking, shouting up the stairway.

"If that damn nurse would check the rest of the first graders' heads, maybe she'd find out where it was really coming from."

"Keep her home then," Marie shouts back.

"Home with who, you? Where's your uncle?"

"I don't know."

Ms. Chavis comes to the bedroom doorway holding the lice comb in her hand. I fix my eyes on the little bits of ink-colored shampoo dripping onto the floor.

"What do you mean, you don't know? Didn't you wait for him?"

"Yeah." Marie takes her hair out of the ponytail she has just made, turns to the mirror and busies herself with putting it up again. "He dropped me off."

"Aw Jesus, Marie, what the hell are you two fighting about again?"

"It's not my fault." Marie kicks the bedroom door shut. "They get on my nerves," she says to me, folding her powwow clothes back into the tissue paper. "If my mom doesn't come back by next year, I'm running away."

Ms. Chavis knocks, "Marie," knocks again, "Marie!"

Marie sits on the edge of the bed and holds her palms against her ears while I listen to Ms. Chavis's muffled footsteps, the noise of her key chain.

"Finish this child's hair, Marie!"

When the screen door slams, I follow Marie out to the kitchen. Shirley is separating clumps of her hair, pulling out eggs. Marie lifts her into the bathtub and rests her head in her palm under the tap. I sit on the toilet. Shirley holds her nose so that her voice sounds silly and nasal.

"I got cooties from Miguel," she says. "He's always trying to kiss me."

"So next time run away, runt."

Marie wrings Shirley's hair out. Syrupy clumps swirl around the drain. When Marie lifts her out, she pouts. "Where's Uncle Jimmy?" She drips water onto the bathroom linoleum, scratches at her head, and begins to cry. Marie presses the towel into her face, pushing hard at her eyes.

"Ow." Shirley smacks at her. "You're hurting me, Marie!"

In the kitchen, Shirley pours soda into a plastic cup full of ice. She pours the soda in carefully, watching the foam fill up and almost spill out of the top of the cup, and then recede. But the bottle slips, and pours out steadily onto the kitchen floor. Shirley sits down in it, holding her emptied cup, and cries. Marie tries to lift her out of the mess so we can clean it up, but Shirley won't budge. She sobs and kicks at Marie. "I hate you," she whines. "I want Uncle Jimmy."

Shirley finally cheers up when she finds she has the hiccups, and we clean up all the soda. Shirley is holding her nose and trying to drink a glass of water at the same time when we hear Jimmy's pickup out front. Shirley bolts to the door. He scoops her up. "You still awake, little woman?" Up high on his hip, Shirley leans her forehead into his and grins. When Shirley's glasses slide down her nose onto his face, she giggles and I feel something sharp like envy. Jimmy sits on the couch and drops his feet on the coffee table, sending a flurry of congealed corned beef hash and paper plates flying onto the carpet. He chugs a whole beer and gives a six-pack to Shirley to put in the refrigerator. He opens another with his key chain. The air bursts out and the cap falls to the floor. I watch as Shirley chases after it.

TWENTY-TWO

The powwow is in San Pedro. We park in a sea of pickups and rusty old cars. Most look pieced together from twenty-year-old parts. There's half a Ford with a VW door screwed and duct-taped on, and a pickup with a bed made from two wooden doors sealed together.

Grand entry doesn't start till two hours later, so Marie and I sit in the grass drinking Coke and eating gummy fry bread while Ms. Chavis sells patches of buckskin, colored ribbons, and crocheted tissue-box covers in the shape of ball gowns, with little doll torsos perched on top. A giant fist points out from Ms. Chavis's T-shirt. FREE LEONARD PELTIER, it shouts. Jimmy sits behind an unadorned wooden frame with nothing to sell. He's breathing heavy in the sun, overweight and overheated, sitting there with a stethoscope and a blood pressure pump around his neck.

"You should have gotten a sign or something," Marie suggests.

Jimmy ignores her. Someone stops by, thinking he is someone else, and shakes his hand.

"Ain't you with the fire circle drummers?"

Jimmy offers his hand. "Healing Bear," he says, "I'm doing blood pressure checks. I'm a medic."

The powwow looks so different from what I remember. The people do not seem magical, not shape-shifters traveling between human and bird. They just look like a bunch of people I don't know. Even the gray feathers, the bright red shawls, the purple headdresses, and elaborate bead designs seem different, manufactured, as if the colors were too bright for nature. The dreary rain is barely visible, but it has made everything vaguely damp and soggy. The powwow booths are all the same color: the dull, institutional gray of hospital walls, painted on thick.

While Marie is dancing, I sit next to Jimmy at his booth. He's many pounds overweight, and I appreciate his heft next to me, the substance of him. When he shifts, the whole long bench rattles. His long hair is the same glossy tar-black as mine, not the pale, soft-butter color of Anne's ponytail, or the wiry blond curls of Mrs. Warrick. When a woman leans over with flyers for us, she says, "Hand that to your dad, honey." I pass it to him. We do look alike. I think of the Warricks, of how desperately I've come to love them, and how guilty it makes me feel. It is not that I do not look like them, it is something else: that in the Warricks' neighborhood, in the school library, in the supermarket, I look like a ghost.

"You think I look Indian?" I ask Jimmy.

"You look like my old uncle," he says. "Now that's a man could dance. You ever learn how to dance Cherokee style? I learned how to dance Cherokee style, all the styles, when I was your age. I could stay at them powwows all day. Everybody would go home without me."

I smile.

In the late afternoon I make my way over to the lawn chairs set up around the dancing area. Marie's aunts, Bettie and Ava, are passing around plates of fry bread and repairing loosened tobacco tops that have fallen off the smallest girls' jingle dresses. Bettie looks me over. "Why don't you want to dance, girl?"

I shrug. "I don't know."

"What happened to your mother?"

"Don't ask her that," Opal says. "You got no right, Ava."

"It's all right," I say. "She went crazy."

"Went crazy?" Opal says. "What are you talking about, child?"

I close my eyes for a moment, try to remember when it started, when I began to understand that she was different from other people. "She started hearing things," I say. "Seeing things that weren't there."

"Visions," Ava says.

"Hush up, Ava," Opal says. "Don't you got nobody else, baby?"

"My grampa," I say. This is the first time I've spoken of him in three years, and my chest goes fluttery. "But he was put in a nursing home."

The aunts shake their heads; a shame, shouldn't work that way, there's nothing to be done.

Marie and Ms. Chavis join us when the men start dancing. Ms. Chavis lights a cigarette. "Is that family decent to you?" she asks.

"They're okay," I say.

"You should be with your own people," Ms. Chavis says.

"What, like you and Uncle Jimmy?" Marie says.

"The child's doing all right if you ask me," Opal says. "She's smart, she's getting to go to a good county school where that can mean something. She's got a roof over her head," Opal glances at Ms. Chavis, "and she's got *two* parents."

"Christ, Opal," Ms. Chavis says. "Would you lay off me for once?"

Opal motions to Jimmy's booth. "What's your man up to over there?"

"He's a paramedic now." Marie rolls her eyes.

"Maybe he'll stick with it," Opal says. "Start treating your poor auntie right."

"Doubtful," Marie says.

Opal offers around a plate of fry bread. "Marie's a half-empty type of person."

"There's nothing in the glass so far as I can see," Marie says.

"Well, the roots *are* deep," Ms. Chavis says. "What's an Indian without his land, that's an Indian without roots, and how the hell can you stand up in the world without your feet planted in something?"

"That ain't it," Opal says. "You girls just inherited the same story we all got. Lemme tell you now, my father, he calls me from some rehab center, from the pay phone where all the sorry-ass Injuns call up their kids and tell them how everything's gonna be different now that they are sober, and all of fifteen minutes! Calls me up and says, 'I'm sorry, you forgive me? I ain't gonna drink no more.' He calls me from that pay phone not four, not five, but six times, and I'm all of eight years old. 'Here I come,' he says. 'I'm coming home to see you, you just wait. Wait for me, now.' So there's me on the steps of our trailer, waiting, because of those goddamn words."

"We learned it from the white man," Ms. Chavis interrupts, "how to use those words. Don't cost you nothing. Just say here, take these horses, we gonna give you all this land and you don't got to worry about nothing. Here, take these blankets, sign right here under these words, here I come, you just wait. Yeah, you just wait until the buffalo start flyin." She leans back in her beach chair and the sun skips across her tar-colored hair. It's so liquid-shiny, the crown of her head actually reflects the sun.

"Hush up, Bettie, would ya?" Opal takes me by the shoulders. "My point is, words are shit. And they're shit because they're everything. Like any magic, they can turn on you."

"Oh for Christ's sake, what has this child got to be so bitter about? Who cares about that crap? You're in a place where you can *go* somewhere, girl. And the bottom line is"—she points at each of the women—"I ain't never heard a none a *you* Injuns going anywhere past the corner bar."

"I am trying to make a home for my niece," Ms. Chavis says, "to make a place she can push off of. She's never wanted for nothing."

"Except a place to come from."

"Why is everyone always talking about the reservation? It ain't nowhere to be proud of, you know. We may have lived there forever, but that don't make the fence any wider. And that's what it is, what it was, and what it always will be." She squeezes her beer can to emphasize her point and throws it toward the bleachers. "A fence."

A terrible silence is spreading out among the dancers. "Oh my God," Opal whispers. The fry bread tumbles out of her lap when she stands. "Jesus, Mary, and Joseph!"

At the top row of benches on the bleachers, a young Indian man is swaying with his eyes closed. He still holds a beer in his hand. He's drifting forward, drifting back, as if in deep, kinetic meditation. Groups of people are running up the stairs toward him, climbing over seats two at a time. A young woman has almost reached him when he tips backward. His hat falls off, bouncing in the grass, and then he follows, doing an entire flip before landing on his back beside the bleachers.

"Christ, he must have passed out." Opal winces, and that is the only thing anybody says until we all watch Jimmy lumbering across the powwow grounds toward the bleachers.

The sun is beginning to go down and they are calling for War Dancers when Jimmy finally returns from the hospital. He has ridden in the ambulance as if he was a relative and Marie wonders out loud what the poor man thought when he came to. People greet Jimmy like he's just scored a touchdown, patting him on the back and walking up to shake his hand. The emcee waves him over and asks him to say a few words to the crowd. Jimmy leans over the microphone and bows his head solemnly.

He says, "The most important thing in the world to me is my people."

I laugh. It all seems so empty, just a mindless ritual echoing something lost. I don't believe any of it. Without Mami, without the match on which to strike the flame, I am mapping and rooting and lighting myself to nowhere.

At the fire circle, I hold hands with the people around me, close my eyes and try to remember why I liked to dance. I remember Mami at powwow. We stood together in the half-light, the faint pink sky turning deep red and dividing the horizon in washes of burnt orange and smoke. It had rained earlier and the drizzle was like an afterthought, steam in the air, like hot water clouds trapped in a bathroom. I wore a jingle dress and held her hand. I jumped to hear the sounds my dress made. I realize it was her face that made me want to dance. It was relaxed and concentrated when she danced, not the taut and downward sloping face she wore at the kitchen table in Papi's trailer. I remember the ashes from her cigarette burning pockmarks in the plastic tablecloth. *Leave me be,* she would say to Papi. *I'm trying to think. Can't you see I'm trying to think?*

I open my eyes when the prayer is over, look around the circle. This is just a show, a cement parking lot on a community college campus. Any memory of the people who lived here, on whose graves they are dancing, is now just gray booths and metal trash cans. It's scraps of buckskin, plastic bins full of turtle shells, Alcoholics Anonymous flyers, and empty beer cans. These turkey feathers, these buckskins and bustles, they are just costumes hiding people.

TWENTY-THREE

Children's Protective Services has a new policy called "transitional counseling sessions." The other foster kids attending the meetings say I'm lucky to have stayed with the Warricks so long. Most of them have been bumped around so often they don't bother to memorize their new addresses and telephone numbers. Since I'm twelve now, I go to group Al-a-Teen meetings, where fourteen of us sit around a grimy room on old torn couches and metal folding chairs, no matter whether we had alcoholic parents or ever had a drink ourselves. When I ask Ms. Garcia about it, she says we're supposed to learn coping mechanisms, that we all come from "a family culture of pain." But the meetings are long and boring. And the counselor is always singling me out. "You need to talk more, Alice. You need to share," he says. "Do you know why you're being kept from your mother? Do you understand the word *schizophrenia*? *Alcoholism*? *Neglect*? How do these words make you feel?"

183

I close my eyes while he talks, pick at the lint on the couch and watch it float down to the floor. The floor is so thick with dirt that when I drag the tip of my shoe across it, it leaves a clean line. Whenever I look at him, he raises his eyebrows and smiles at me blandly. He has a ponytail, though he's bald on top, and his tennis shoes are bright, bright white.

At the break I buy a soda with the money Mrs. Warrick has given me for the vending machine and go outside to sit on the curb. Most kids go outside to light cigarettes and I like to watch the whirl of smoke that twirls up from their huddle. It's early evening and the streetlights are just coming on. A group of boys gather around the phone booth in a huddle. I'm watching the brilliant sky-colors burning through the clouds when one of them calls to me.

"What's your name?" I count four of them, all staring. The one who asked is looking me up and down, the traverse of his eyes making a shudder begin at my thighs and roll through me in a peculiar ache. He's tall and lanky, his long black hair loose around his shoulders. A face of angles and narrow lines like Papi's. He wears jeans, a red T-shirt with a decal of an eagle on it.

"Alice," I say, and then I'm suddenly embarrassed that I've said so. Is Alice a weird name?

"I'll see you around, Alice." He turns, laughs into the huddle of boys, and breathes into a plastic bag full of thick white glue.

At the next group meeting, I can't help staring at the slippery-looking black hair knotted at the nape of his neck. At the break, he

184

stays inside instead of going out to smoke, and follows me to the vending machine.

"Hey," he says, a half-smile forming, "I know you."

I bow my head; drop my quarters into the machine. "Hey."

He says, "What kinda Indian are you?"

"Quechan, I guess. Maybe Diegueño, Aymara, too."

"I'm Papago. My dad lives in Sedona, but my mom's easier to get along with, so I came up here. You in foster?"

I nod. How can he tell?

"I was in foster for a while, but then my mom got us back when she went to AA. My sister lives with my gramma in Sedona. I'm glad though, I mean about my sister. She's really prissy."

I lean against the vending machine, fold my arms across my chest.

He says, "You're pretty."

He looks so bony. His skin is the color of a new burn, his hair a melting tar color.

I smile. He says, "You want to see something cool?"

We walk together down the wide streets, stop in a liquor store for cigarettes and a new lighter, then take a bus. There are more Indians on the streets, and we pass the neighborhood where Grampa's house was. I took Marie to Grampa's house once and we saw a Mexican family with four little girls playing outside. Next door, the neighbors were being evicted. All their stuff was piled up in the alley and around the front door: a sofa, a high chair, a half empty chest of drawers. There was a spilled trash bag and clothes and diapers scattered down the street. I looked for Mami in the faces outside the bars, the homeless people pushing carts that looked like her, their clothes piled on, their plastic bags and bundles around them like a moat. Whenever I saw long black hair or a woolen stocking cap, I hoped it was her.

Mannie leads me to a long alleyway beside a boarded-up bar called The Neon Coyote. The alley is like any other, filled with discarded beer bottles and a few needles. But the walls are covered with graffiti; even some places on the ground are marked by tribal symbols, animal markings, and signatures. Mannie points to one of the signatures.

Red Power!

Jimmy Rodriguez

1968

He traces the name. "That's my uncle. No shit though, he told me about this place. It's Indian land, right? They claimed this alley." He laughs, puts a heavy arm around me. "It's your home away from home."

I hardly ever see my new social worker. Ms. Garcia used to drop in at odd times, at school or at meetings, but the new one doesn't even remember my name. She has to look over her files whenever I see her, sort out who I am and where I've come from. She doesn't notice when I cut school or skip group counseling. I leave school on the regular counseling pass and then meet up with Mannie and

Marie. I take the bus back in the early afternoon and then get on the school bus home. We hang out at the empty warehouses or the scrap yard. Marie meets me at the bus stop and we walk the three blocks to the junkyard and climb under the fence. Mannie and the other boys make friends with the dog. They feed it scraps of pork fat and scratch behind its ears, giving it our jackets to smell. It lets us climb under the fence and walk straight through the corrugated metal gates as if we belong there. And we climb up into a smashed yellow school bus that sags into a small hill of mud and scraps. The boys hang out around the steering wheel, sniffing glue and working on busted wires from old batteries and car radios. Marie shakes up a can of whipped cream, inhales it, and makes us all laugh singing "Staying Alive" in a cartoon voice and dancing on the torn vinyl seats.

The boys have bought the newspaper because Enrique's name is in the Metro section, listed under local juvenile offenses for stabbing another boy and for stealing forty ounces of beer from a truck unloading at the liquor store. They are huddled around the paper when Enrique says, "I'm fuckin' famous."

"Hey, don't curse," the older boy says in a teacher voice. "There is a child present." They look at me and laugh.

"Marie's little sidekick? She can't help it. She's learning how to be a white girl."

Marie says, "Shut up already. At least she ain't a thief."

"Check it out, man." Enrique spreads the paper out on the steering wheel. "It's that old lady's fire."

"It's so sad." Marie lies down on one of the bench seats, her feet dangling out the window. "That old woman was cool."

"Mannie saw the fire trucks, three of them. It just happened last night."

"I saw the roof go, it caved in on itself, made this crazy smacking sound."

I lean in toward Mannie, and he smiles.

"I saw them carrying out the old woman. Two of the firemen dragged her out and the others ran up and put her on a stretcher."

"It was crazy. One minute an old green house with a porch and that lady's garden and the next it's all roaring like a couple a logs in a fireplace. All that spraying from the trucks just made all these big puffs and clouds of smoke. And you look at it now, it's like somebody pulled the roof off, stuck their hand in and scraped everything out."

Later, when they're all getting drunk and smacking bottles against a turned-over Camaro, Mannie and I play with the dog.

"How come the owner's never here?"

"He only comes in on Mondays and Wednesdays."

I tug on the dog's ears and look up at Mannie nervously. "I want to see the burned-out house."

The fire is new enough that the frame and the pieces of furniture and scattered dishes that survived are covered in a fine gray ash that feels like milled powder when I rub it between my index finger and thumb. Though it's only late afternoon outside, the inside rooms of the house are pitch black, the windows opaque with ash or covered in debris. We wander the rooms together, Mannie holding a lighter above us that casts a tiny triangle, revealing pieces of wall and fallen ceiling beams. Everywhere, there is cracked plaster and broken glass, wood beams that have turned to hollow strips of black. I love, especially, the televisions and stereos, melted into new shapes that look like poured wax.

"She must have died right away," Mannie says. "When they brought her out she was in a nightgown." We walk around the bedroom. There is a pink plastic brush melted into a dresser that sags toward the floor, a picture frame, and two blackened curlers. "Have you ever seen a dead person?" Mannie says.

"Yeah. I've been to a funeral."

"No, like just dead."

"No."

"I did. My uncle overdosed. He was on the floor already dead when the ambulance came."

"What did he look like?"

"Like sleeping."

"How did you know he was dead?"

"All my aunties and uncles were crying, yelling at each other."

He lights a cigarette and hands it to me, but just having it hover close to my mouth reminds me of Mami. I inhale quickly, blow it all out at once.

I think about the old woman. "What do you think happens when you're dead?"

"Nothing, you're just dead."

And then I say this, though it makes no sense. "My mother is dead." As soon as I've said it, I am flooded with panic. It could be true; I don't know where she is. I feel as if whatever connected us is gone. It has been a long time since I have thought of my words as incantations, yet I fear them, and think of Mami's hands above me. *Careful, baby, careful.* Or maybe it's because I now know I am going forward without her to a world unsanctified. And I am shaking, sweat and cold waves flooding my back and neck and tears hot on my cheek and neck, burning my eyes and making me struggle for breath. Mannie opens one side of his jean jacket like a bird wing, folds me in. And I stay there for a while, feeling his heart race against my cheek, his bony arm around my waist.

Though I'm careful crossing the puzzle of beams on the floor, I fall through, landing on soft dirt and exposed floorboards. Mannie holds the lighter down near me for a moment and it flicks off when he bends to grab my arms. Then he leans in and kisses me. The wetness surprises me. I do not move, but slow down inside. The world expands, things go quiet around me. I pull away and try to slow my breath.

"Listen, I'm sorry." His hands are on my face. "I didn't mean nothing by it."

But I do not want it to stop, the world lit up again and blazing. I pull him into me. The raw-wood floor beams press a pattern of splinters into my thighs. And his breath is hot on my neck. His mouth is insistent and I draw all of it in at once, in one long inhale, close my eyes and his hands are on me, urgent fingers everywhere. I rock inward, slow down, breathe deep. For this moment, for now, I want to give, to open up and pull him in. I want to love the scars on his mouth and wrist, his oily black eyes; the damp curls around his temples, his crooked teeth. I do not know myself.

TWENTY-FOUR

A few days after my fourteenth birthday, Mr. Warrick calls me into the kitchen, away from where I lay on the couch with Anne. She's been painting my toenails. Before I can get up, she blows on my feet, fans them with her hands, and then rips away the tissue she has wound around my toes to separate them. Mrs. Warrick is sitting at the table, cradling a cup of coffee in her palms. Her face is drawn and tired.

I see it right away on the breakfast counter: a fat, padded manila envelope. A stack of paper wrapped in rubber bands, ragged and brown around the edges, full of the promise of artifacts. I've believed since I came here in this kind of promise: that I might draw a map of my life, around the holes inside me, and follow them home, follow them back to that place where I started. But slowly, I begin to understand what it means: why else would official things with a government stamp arrive for me? I don't think the words *I have lost her.*

193

Instead I think of the rules for algebraic equations; simplifying, the acronyms meant to nudge my memory when it is lazy, not grasping and desperate like this. I think, PEMDAS—parentheses, exponents, multiplication, division.

"Oh," I whisper. "Okay." Then the dishes. "It's my turn, isn't it?" We all know it is not. Yet I go and stand by the sink, and it is quiet and I think of numbers and not of the burning in my ears. I turn on the water, lift a glass, make circles with soap on a sponge, and it is there still, on the table behind me. I had time. I thought I could go back to her, be hers again before she was gone like this.

Mrs. Warrick comes to stand beside me. She takes the plate from my hands, unfurls the rag from my fist, and gives me the package. I lock the door to our bedroom and dump the envelope out onto my bed: foster parent papers; enrollment forms; birthday cards written on hospital stationery; letters written to me, but not stamped or addressed. Then her hospital records. I add them up precisely, all the evidence of days spent in buildings with names like Green Grove and Shepherd's Refuge, using my school calculator. Six hundred and forty-one days. Then the number and variety of treatments: cold therapy, so odd and cheerful-sounding, as if a brisk walk in the winter would knock it out of her; shock therapy; a long list of unpronounceable drugs; wrapping; vocational rehabilitation; life skills; Sunday trips to church. There is a vaccination certificate from Compton Indian Free Clinic, a photograph, a shell fragment, a pow-wow flyer. There is a picture of Mami at the Bureau of Indian Affairs

School, quiet-eyed and smiling, her hands folded neatly on her desk. I wonder if this picture is from before she started crying, before she started drinking, as if all those tears were just whiskey and six-packs soaking through. But these *are* just relics. There is nothing vital or fleshy here, nothing to hold on to.

The papers are like a voice over the phone. I put them down gently, then yank open the dresser and rip up the maps I've drawn. I tear down pictures, take down the atlases and fling them at the closet, try hard to rip the pages from my book of buried cities. I open the window, light up a Polaroid of Anne and me, and watch it curl away. My past reaches out for me, knocks me off my feet and leaves me facedown on the bedroom floor, trying to catch my breath between sobs. I lie there on the floor for a while, until I begin to remember her. But what I remember are the times we turned away from each other. A memory of myself near the creek ignoring her; she calls from the screen door of Papi's trailer: *Alice, Al, come in.* I am washing the shell of a hermit crab that Papi brought me, dipping it in the water and easing the smudges off with my thumb. My fingers are growing numb in the cold water. *Al, angel, come in.* But I move slowly, jump each step like the drawn blocks of hopscotch.

At the top of the step, I stop and ask her what's wrong. "Are you lonely?"

"It's not safe out there," she says.

From the screen door, I turn to look outside, sniff the air. "What," I ask, "where?"

"All around," she says. "Everywhere."

I hold my hand up, make her pinkie-swear. "Promise we won't leave."

And later, inside that ambulance on the day we lost each other. I lean into her chest, try to match my breath to the pace of her fingers raking my back through the T-shirt. She's scratching too hard. I wonder what she saw, in the park, that I could not. I imagine she was lost inside one of Sister Joanne's stories. We were not in a park in Los Angeles, in a toilet stall. We were in a red desert, our hair knotted into braids, our bodies similar. We did not look like ourselves. We looked like two white peasant women. And in the basin, Mami washed the crown of Christ. She tried to clean the blood from the braided thorns he wore on his head. Little splinters of twigs settled on the porcelain. When she lifted her hands out of the basin, her fingers had grown cuts. She kissed my bloody hands. I imagine it wasn't until she looked up at the door that she saw how we looked. The basin was a dirty public restroom, the sand just grimy tile.

Home is with Mami. But I gave her up. With my eyes closed, I see it clearly: in a sterile-smelling hospital room, the curtain is drawn, and the lights are painfully bright.

"Is she going to be okay?" Mami asks the pretty doctor.

"Yes," the doctor says. "Yes, she is going to be fine."

I turn my head away from Mami, hold the doctor tight. When she tries to hand me to Mami, I curl my nails into the fleshy skin above her elbows. I won't let go.

"Is this your daughter?" the policeman asks.

Mami's eyes are clear, watching me. She gives me what I've asked for. "No," she decides. She fingers the bruises on my arm. "No, she's no relation at all."

In a space on a hospital form, the doctor has written "referral to soc. services." I think about the pretty doctor, bent over her papers and signing me away, signing the logical complaint, fitting us into the constructions of reason. How did my mother look to her? Did Mami even see my dirty undershirt sticking to me, did she notice there in the hospital, where it was too late for her notice to count, that the ruby-colored rings on my cheeks were raw like the insides of a grapefruit? I squeezed her hand; I pressed my forehead into her hips. And then the nurses tugged gently, unraveling me like a thread on a sweater. This doctor, scanning her papers, did she examine it this way? Did she weigh it on her forms under the sections marked "Comments, Observations"? Did she enter under "Diagnosis," the words *loss, separation, betrayal*? Did she make red marks under "Recommendations" that said sanctify, mend, connect?

I stuff everything back in the envelope, take the tiny shell and go outside to the pool, where the birds of paradise are making shadows on the water, and wash it. The shell cleans nicely; a speckled brown surface emerges. Mrs. Warrick and Anne have fallen asleep on the hammock, their arms wrapped around each other, cheeks touching, hands linked, their faces drawn in to each other. That shape that their arms make in the space between them is home. And they can erect it any time they want. Anywhere, they can make home. But I don't fit in that shape.

Back behind the quiet house, behind the sleeping Warricks where the dirt is moist and pliable, I dig out my T-shirt. It is grayed and filthy. I hold it against my face, searching for her smell. I'm tired. Mami was right. It's so hard to *be* someplace. Be *here,* for instance. I'm good at coming and going. I won't even really miss anyone when I go. The truth is I don't know how to live in this house. I never figured out how to unpack, how to make a place here. This family feels temporary, a blanket I crawled under in the cold. Anne goes to ballet classes and band rehearsal. She wears her fine hair pulled back the same way her mother does. Her eyes recede in the same way when she grins. But I'm like a visitor every day, walking through the house, spying on these people I've been trying to love. And they are always looking back at me, not with recognition, but something else, a look that passes over me, resting on my dark eyes and black hair as if I were a cat carried in from the street. They love me, sure, but not like they love one another. I want to *have* a place, to come from somewhere. I want to be able to stand up with the people I love and say this is who I am. I've been trying the Warricks on like clothes. *I am a foster child,* I say, *a Warrick.* But they don't fit. Mami was the condor. I was the young girl. I hid under the trailer, waiting to be carried off to the ears of the mountain. She came up with all sorts of ways to trick me into coming out. Her voice, an echo in the dark space: I'll feed you, little skinny girl. Come here. Aren't you hungry?

TWENTY-FIVE

The problem, I've decided, has to do with blood. If I can't have Mami, then I want Papi. I've brought the contents of my package, my sweatshirts, and the map I've made of the world underneath California, the places in the deserts and coastlines where pottery was removed or stolen, where graves were turned over, revealing entire ghost worlds. I've drawn all the caves and shelters where people lived, copied the writings on the walls. I've read about the bones found near the reservation, I've got a picture in my pocket. It shows the scattered bones and pieces of skeleton where they rest in the dirt, found on a hill outside the reservation. Pieces have been sent to a university museum in San Diego. I remember the bird bones, the sweaty faces of men digging and moving rocks. "Your gramma's gramma," Sister Joanne said. *You're digging up cousins. Ghosts in the fire.* If people travel home, back to Avikwaamé in the smoke, then these bones are unchanged, trapped in the earth.

201

• • •

I stand on the highway out past the Greyhound station, hold my arm out, thumb up. A few swishing lights pass me by, blasting my hair with wind. Finally, a Mack truck with a swaying trailer pulls off ahead of me, and backs down the shoulder slowly. When I walk around to the cab, a man leans over and opens the passenger-side door. "Hey," he says, pushing a red mesh baseball cap up high on his forehead. "What are you doing out here in the middle of the night all alone?"

I shrug.

"It's not safe out here, you in trouble or something?"

"I'm trying to get home," I say.

He looks at me intently. "And where's that?"

"Yuma," I say.

"Yuma! Jesus, that's six hours easy."

I shift my backpack.

"Well, come on," he says, motioning for me to come up into the cab. I pull the door shut and the light in the cab eclipses the dark outside.

"How old are you?" he asks.

"Eighteen." I can tell he doesn't believe it, but he nods, looking me over, and flicks off the overhead light.

He messes with the radio a bit, then looks me over again. "So what are you doing way out here?"

I shrug and he doesn't push it. I'm asleep fast, my head rocking on the chilled window, music purring softly from the truck radio. When I wake the first light is just coming up pink and orange on the horizon, and I am surprised at how the changing landscape outside looks so familiar. Some of the hills are blackened from recent fires, the brown and red patches marked by fields of black or bright green regrowth.

By eight o'clock, we're in Quartzite, an enormous desert rest stop of campers and filling stations. He pulls into the truck stop and turns the ignition off. The truck does a little shimmy before quitting. He lights a cigarette, offers the pack to me.

"Don't smoke?" he asks. "Good, nasty habit for a girl." He holds my eyes, looks me over slowly, down to my legs and then back up again slowly till he's caught my eyes again. I look away, out at the light-studded darkness. Fast-food signs, rotating gas marquees, a sad-looking desert darkness.

He buys a brown shopping bag full of beer from the gas station and hands me one. I drink it down, the whole can, and he laughs. He opens another and hands it to me. My head is starting to lighten, my shoulders and neck gone tingly. He leans over and my hand goes up automatically. He laughs again, taking my wrist in his hand.

The next two beers go down warm and sour, and my throat tightens. The lights outside are melting, the inside of the cab going fuzzy and whirling.

"So, what are you doing out here all alone?"

"I'm going home," I say. "I told you."

"Home to who? You got a boyfriend?"

"Home to who?" I can't get my mouth around the words. "Home to who?"

I let him press his lips to mine, cold lips wet from the beer. They taste like smoke. When I kissed Mannie, I felt as if there might be some place between us, in that shape that our arms made around each other, that I could call home. But there was nothing there. There's no home out here.

"My mother is the mountain," I say. "She has river veins and molten blood. My father is Kwikumat, but he doesn't make daughters, he makes whole tribes."

The man laughs again. I feel his hand on my thigh.

"Isn't that funny?" I laugh. "Isn't that really just fucking funny?"

He opens another beer for me.

I drink it down. "You want to hear a story?"

"Sure," he says, "I want to hear a story." He runs his hands gently across my cheek.

"When I was a little girl," I say.

"Such a pretty little girl," he says.

"I met a condor."

"A what?"

"A condor. You know," I hold my arms out wide, "a bird, big and black. And he said to me, are you hungry, little girl?"

He giggles, tries to pour a beer into my mouth. It dribbles down my shirt. He says, "Are you thirsty, little girl?"

"So the condor stole me."

"Aww," he says.

"Flew me to the top of the mountain and kept me there until my grandmother found me and hid me in a barrel. When the condor discovered this," I say, "he pecked at the barrel, pecked and pecked until all that was left of me was dry bones."

"Shit, baby," the man says.

I roll down the window, lean my head out into the cold night air. "Dry bones!" I scream, listening to my echo over the noise of insects.

He slides his fingers across my midriff, slipping his thumb underneath the fabric. I open the door, but he takes my wrist and squeezes tightly, smiling.

"Where you off to?" he says. "Ain't you thirsty no more, little girl?"

I hold his gaze for a few minutes, trying to decide. I could keep going, I could stop, I could be, do, anything. I could be her, I could be my mother.

I climb out of the cab and walk around to the front of the truck, lean against the quitted headlight. The alcohol makes my head swim. I take a few steps forward—all blurry, empty desert, swaying and refocusing—then I am still and everything is swirling.

Home is with Mami. But I understand the truth now. I gave her up.

"Where am I?" I sob.

He says Quartzite, working his hand down my jeans.

I knee him. I'm halfway across the road, when I see lights flicking, pulling over for me.

TWENTY-SIX

It is strange traveling the same route Mami and I first went together. Even stranger that I remember the route exactly, right down to the number of the bus and the exact turns on the road once I get off at the bar, and then from the bar, up the gravel road to the reservation. It is a memory like a photograph, floating in watery longings. I find Papi's trailer without hesitation, but everything seems a little different, smaller, quieter, no hippies, no campfires. Papi is sitting on the trailer steps, drinking from a cooler of beer that sits on the scorched grass beside him, where Mami's little molehills of put-out cigarettes used to form. I spend a moment thinking about how I might dig through the grass and dirt and uncover the relics, the butts of cigarettes, and how, examining each one, I might know something about her, use them like artifacts to light on who she was.

Papi looks up at me and turns almost instantly white.

"Jesus Christ, I thought you were Amalie."

"I'm Alice." I wait a moment; smile awkwardly. "Papi."

He smiles too. He's a little drunk, his eyes all sleepy like when I first met him. "You look just like her. What are you doing here?"

I try to think of how to answer when Papi interrupts, "Is Lee with you?"

"No, I think she might be . . . I got this form that said 'freed for adoption,' and . . . we were staying with Grampa. He died. Since we left here—" I drop my backpack onto the gravel, it seems like too much to explain. "I thought, you know, since Mami's gone, I should come back to my father."

Papi swallows an entire bottle of beer before he answers.

"You're not mine, Alice."

"What?"

"How old are you?"

"Thirteen."

"So you were . . . five when you came here, and I hadn't seen Lee in eight years."

"But, you were—" I'm not sure what I'm going to say.

I sit next to him, and he hands me a bottle. He flips the cap off, the air rushes out, and the beer goes down cold and sour.

"Your mother." He smiles, looks tired. "Something, huh? God, she ruined me."

"Sorry."

"Don't be." He laughs then, looking ahead. "Without her, there wouldn't have been any me to ruin." I follow his eyes, half expecting to see Mami walk up the gravel road and sit down with us.

"Is she making out all right?"

"No, not really. I mean, you know, she's been sick?"

He doesn't answer, but turns and looks me up and down as if seeing me for the first time. "How'd you get here?"

"Bus."

"And you said you were staying where?"

"I didn't. I thought I would—"

He kicks my foot lightly. "You run away?"

But before I can answer, he says, "You must be hungry." He picks up my backpack, and holds the screen door open for me. Inside looks just the same, everything brown and worn down, and fans jimmied into every window.

"Let's see," Papi says. He looks in the cupboards, opens up all the drawers, opens the refrigerator twice, but all he has is beer and a half-eaten bowl of ramen noodles.

"I wish I had some potatoes." He scratches the back of his neck, looks at me through embarrassed half-closed eyes. "You still love french fries?"

I weep, but quietly.

He holds his arms open and I fold myself into his hug.

"Just because you don't belong here," he whispers, "don't mean you don't belong nowhere."

Anywhere, I think. *I don't belong anywhere.*

209

. . .

He calls the Warricks and Anne answers the phone. "Where are you?" she whispers. I can hear her voice wavering. "You better come h—" I close my hand over the phone, hang up before she says it.

We go to the liquor store first where Papi tries to get them to cash his check. When they won't do it, we go to Lenny's and borrow fifty dollars from the bartender. He tells Papi to hit up Lou.

Lou is an old woman at the end of the bar taking sips from a glass of beer into which she keeps spooning clumps of ice.

"What you need it for?"

"I got to give someone a ride home."

She stirs the ice around in her beer. Then she turns to look at me.

"I only got twenty."

"It's a long way," Papi says.

"Well, then you got to be resourceful. You know Lester Pride's mother? She won at bingo last night. You better go ask her."

But before we leave, Lou smacks the shoulder of an old drunk next to her. His hand slips off his cheek and his hat wobbles. "Give the man some money," she says.

He turns to face us, but his eyes stay fixed on Lou.

"What you lookin' at?" she asks him. "We all know you're blind as a bat."

"What? I'm just gonna give away money 'cause you said so? Don't I ought to know who I'm dealing with?"

She smacks him again, but he holds on to his hat.

"All right, but it ain't for him, it's for her." He smiles wide. "She smells like Jean Naté."

"What?"

"I buy it for my daughter every year on her birthday."

"Cheap bastard," Lou says.

"Thanks, Lou." Papi kisses her on the cheek.

"Papi, wait." I grab his arm outside the bar. I stare up at the neon sign on Lenny's door front. *It's dead,* I keep thinking, staring up at it stupidly, *it's dead.*

In bed that night on the same pilled and stained plaid couch that I slept on so many years ago, I think about my vision. The condor that followed me to Grampa's but would not come when I wished for it in bed next to Anne.

Here, on the reservation, the old people say that we come from the mountains. The mountain is a womb, made of river veins and molten blood. But I don't believe I come from the mountains. I come from my father and he was not anyone.

TWENTY-SEVEN

The quiet here keeps me awake. It is dark, much darker than in the city when I walk out of the trailer's screen door, and down the gravel path. I head for the hill, for the bones growing out of it. The old mounds are marked off since the museum bought the land. The dig is now outside the reservation's boundaries, though separated only by this hill.

With a rock from the path leading up to the dig, I break the window of the main research building. I expect an alarm, but there is none, just the tremendous smacking sound of glass breaking. The glass shatters into various pieces, each containing its own delicate network of cracks and circular bursts, like bubbles in water. I wait for lights to come on over the hill, but no one seems to have heard. It takes awhile to clear away the glass so I can climb through the window.

Inside, I run my hands along the mud blocks and pottery shards assembled on the light tables. I dig through the filing cabinets, removing flat files and pottery shards, unlabeled artifacts and dozens of rolled-up maps. They are surprisingly light, all undisturbed for so long that they leave fine sprays of dust on my fingers. A strong wind comes through the shattered window and scatters the papers around the floor. Among them are labeled diagrams, imagined maps of an entire Hohokan city reconstructed using all of this digging and longing and imagining.

This is what I find: an *olla,* a repository for the dust of a burial fire; an unfinished basket, the juncus leaves ragged and fanned; maps; surveys of the area; reconstructions; blueprints with numbers labeling the locations of stone tools pulled out of the dirt. I stuff the maps into my backpack, bundle the pottery and baskets into a tablecloth from the small kitchen area, and push them through the broken window.

Outside, some makeshift wooden poles with bright yellow tape tied between them connect the various mounds. It is on the third mound, partitioned off separately with numbered stakes, that I find the bones I'm looking for. They are just like their picture, scattered pieces emerging slightly, a head tilted up sadly, as if trapped there, waiting for me.

I begin to collect leaves, make a bed two feet deep on top of the sunken bones. The wind is strong on the hill. It lifts my hair, and whips it around, lashing my cheeks. It picks up dry brush and a few light twigs and tosses them around in the moonlight. It takes much longer than I expect. I have to make several trips with my arms full of brush from the slash piles in order to fill it. But when I've made a fair pyre, I begin on the poles, arranging them around the grave like the support beams of a house.

I hunt around the area for fallen branches, cut them with one of Papi's kitchen knives. It helps that the beetles have worked on them. The dried bark stripped from the mesquite and the branches of willow tear easily, like old dried-out newspaper. Once I've gotten all of the wood standing, I drop my old world map on the pile, take off my jacket, and cover it. I add the ribbons from Mami's turtle shawl and a knot of hair from the bottom of my braid. Then more dried leaves and bark until the mound is filled over and spread out on the dry ground beyond the grave. Some of the leaves are carried off in the wind and I watch them float up and whirl around in the moonlight.

It is really just the smallest of sparks that begins it. I light a slip of blueprint paper and watch it curl around a twig. The end of it glows. Then I drop it onto the grave, into the tangled nest of arrowweeds. The twig rocks in the breeze among the piled-together leaves and I add my breath. I fan it with my fingers. The turned-over mud and debris is damp, and gives in reluctantly, waning lazily, in some places blinking out entirely before sparking up again. Still, it seems slight encouragement for the fire that grows to the height of my knee, and moves rapidly, sparking on the nettles and dry grasses that cover the surrounding ground.

I kneel and try to pray, to sing, but I don't know any songs, not

even a prayer. When I close my eyes I see my mother, my grandfather, spinning wheels and spools, my own bones and flesh.

I dump the contents of my backpack out around the grave,
arranging them like coordinates on a timeline. A photograph, a crab
shell, a birth certificate. I place them at each corner of the structure
I've built, weighted down by small blocks of mud. Artifacts of paper,
blue mimeographs written in the peculiar jargon of 1960s psychia-
try, foster parent reports and hospital forms. I wrap Mami's picture
in the Paleolithic wall maps, the time and place where Kwikumat
and his dust and water began, where the vestiges of civilization were
gathering momentum, and I bury it at the east pole. And finally, with
my map spread out around me, I toss each relic into the fire, and listen to its story.